THORNBOUND

Volume II of The Harwood Spellbook

STEPHANIE BURGIS

Five Fathoms Press

DEDICATION

For Rene Sears and Jenn Reese, who have beta-read and cheered me on through so many first drafts and scary new ventures. I appreciate you both so much!

It was bad enough to be deprived of my new husband before our wedding night. It was utterly unjust to be tormented by nightmares weeks afterward as I slept, *still* alone, in our marital bed.

For the ninth morning in a row, I woke up gasping and clawing at my throat, fighting to yank piercing thorns out from my skin...thorns that, of course, existed nowhere but in my dreams.

Groaning, I tipped my head back against my pillow. Darkness filled the un-curtained windows across from me, with no hints of dawn yet to illuminate the thick woodland beyond. Still, I knew better than to make any reckless attempts to fall back to sleep. There was only one dream I ever experienced nowadays, and it would suck me directly back into its maw if I allowed my eyes to fall shut again.

It was exhausting, infuriating, and an irony beyond compare for the headmistress of Angland's first women's college of magic to be the only magician in the nation who couldn't cast a simple spell to protect her sleep. I had lost my own magic over nine months ago, though, and Wrexham's pillow—which had been placed so hopefully beside mine on the morning of our wedding five weeks earlier—was still depressingly empty and unused. He had been called away by an urgent messenger in the middle of our wedding breakfast, and he still hadn't returned from the latest wild goose chase that he'd been sent on by the Boudiccate.

Of course, their messages always claimed that no other officer of magic could be trusted with any of those vital missions that had disrupted every day he'd reserved to spend with me after our wedding...but the message behind that endless stream of summonses was unmistakable. Those powerful, elegant women who collectively ruled our nation were anything but subtle in their indications of displeasure —and although my late mother had once led their number, I myself was now officially their least favorite constituent.

Groaning, I pushed my bedcovers aside and forced myself upright, fighting through the sticky cobweb of exhaustion and leftover dread that that hateful dream always left in its wake. In the unrelenting darkness, it was too easy to remember the inescapable, choking helplessness I'd felt, *again*, as thorn-covered vines wound around my throat and mouth and—

No. My teeth clenched as I slammed my bare feet onto the cold wooden floorboards, drawing strength from the shock of contact. I had been fighting against the Boudiccate's stifling disapproval and the age-old rules of our society ever since I'd first discovered my own gift for magic decades ago. I would hardly let a few bad dreams—or lovesickness—slow me down at this most crucial moment of my life.

Today my groundbreaking school of magic for women— the brilliant, nation-shaking project that I desperately hoped to make my great life's work—was *finally* due to open its doors, after months of vicious newspaper attacks and political obstruction. My students—nine bright, shining young women full of potential—would start arriving before noon, along with their nervous parents and—I devoutly hoped—the final member of my own newly-hired staff, just in time for the first classes to begin tomorrow.

Everything had to be perfect for their arrival.

But I was caught hopelessly off-guard after all, by the news that my politician sister-in-law brought me six hours later, when she found me kneeling in my warm, cozy library of magic, re-ordering two different sections of books—*again*—with a trail of empty teacups and saucers spread across the rich green and silver carpet beside me.

"What do you mean, the Boudiccate have *changed their minds?*" I demanded.

I stared up at Amy, still holding a stack of books in my hands and caught between horror and disbelief. I'd consumed at least half a dozen cups of tea since I'd arisen, using my extra waking hours to double- and triple-check every final inspection, but exhaustion still clung to my bones. "They finally gave us their blessing—"

"The Boudiccate gave you their *permission*," Amy corrected me grimly, "and only with extreme reluctance. Now, however..." She held up the letter she'd carried into the library. "They've been provided," she said, "with new and 'compelling' arguments regarding the dangers of this enterprise, all of which must be fully considered—and can, apparently, only be decided upon after an in-person inspection."

"An—?" Shaking my head, I pushed myself up from the carpeted floor to look at my sister-in-law more carefully.

A mere two months after giving birth to my first niece, Amy's beautiful, beloved dark brown face was lined with all

STEPHANIE BURGIS

of the exhaustion that might be expected in a new mother, especially one so unconventional—not to mention stubborn —as to insist upon feeding her child herself. Considering that she had, in addition, persisted in aiding me in my own work even with a nursing infant frequently clasped in her arms, it was no wonder that there were deep shadows lurking beneath her eyes now.

But I glimpsed more than simple exhaustion in her face. There was an unhappy turn to her lips, and her warm brown eyes looked strained with more than tiredness.

For the past five weeks, ever since my painfully abbreviated wedding day, I'd clamped a firm lid on my emotions, throwing every bit of my energy into the final stages of creating my school—and into its vigorous defense against each fresh onslaught of offensive public and private opinion and last-minute administrative hurdles.

Now, though, I looked hard at Amy and frowned. "Something's amiss," I said. "Shouldn't you have had notice of this change in the wind far earlier? Your friends in the Boudiccate—"

"Oh, this letter made it *quite* clear that they're no longer sharing sensitive information with me." Amy waved one hand dismissively, as if we were discussing trivialities rather than her life's work. "You needn't concern yourself, Cassandra. I knew from the outset that they wouldn't be pleased about your school. I made the choice to support you anyway."

And I had been surprised that she'd found so much free time to help me with it. Now I narrowed my eyes at her. "I specifically recall you telling me you were only taking a temporary leave of absence from your political duties for little Miranda's first months."

"I was." Amy gave a careless shrug. "But it appears—

4

based on this letter—that my absence from politics may last longer than I'd anticipated. Never mind. Perhaps it's time for me to find a new vocation, as you did."

Her expression was perfectly, purposefully serene, but Amy had been my older sister in all but blood for over fifteen years now, and she'd been strategizing toward a place in the Boudiccate all her life. I'd been certain that this was the year she would finally win that place.

A new seat had opened in the Boudiccate five months ago, for the first time in years. There could be no question that she was the best-qualified politician available to fill it.

"I cannot believe you didn't tell me they were threatening to sanction you!" Tossing my stack of books aside, I strode across the carpeted floor of the library. Amy herself had helped me decorate the room two weeks ago, whilst laughing and chatting and distracting me from all of my own minor anxieties.

"You know I would never ask you to choose my career over yours!" I said. "I would have done all of this without you if I'd known—you could have pretended to disapprove! I would have found a different home for the school, far away from our family, so that you could officially disavow me, and—"

"*Cassandra*." The iron in Amy's voice cut me off. "It is done," she said quietly. "I know you would never ask me to make that choice, but *they did*. And if you think I would ever choose anything above my family..."

Silence fell as my shoulders sagged in acceptance. Of course Amy would never make that choice. She was the acknowledged and adored matriarch of our clan, the rock that kept us safe through every storm.

"Is it too late?" I asked finally. "If I move the school now..." Involuntarily, I glanced toward the window; all those hopeful girls traveling across the nation to join us as we spoke, after so many months of tooth-grinding negotiations and so many painstaking arrangements....

Still. I would send them all back without a twinge if it would save my sister-in-law's future.

"Far too late," Amy said firmly. "Trust me. The ultimatum that the Boudiccate gave me in their last letter was entirely explicit. I'd hoped that I might persuade them to see reason, but apparently, all of my arguments have failed. So..." Her lips twisted. "Let's make certain this school is a success, shall we?"

"Indeed." My chest tightened even as I gave her a firm nod.

This school *had* to succeed, now more than ever. It wasn't only a matter of my satisfaction, or even of hers; it was a point that had to be proven for the sake of every magic-loving woman who came after us.

For over seventeen hundred and fifty years, ever since the great Boudicca herself had sent the Romans fleeing Angland with the help of her second husband's magery, a clearly defined line had been drawn in the public arena, never to be broken. The hard-headed ladies of Angland saw to the practicalities of rule whilst the more mystical and emotional gentlemen dealt with magic. Together, they had worked for centuries to hold our nation strong against invasions and threats without ever crossing that agreed-upon line...

Until me.

I had been the first woman student ever admitted to the Great Library of Trinivantium to study magic. Afterward, I had been Angland's only known woman magician for years —until I had lost all my ability to cast magic in an experiment of overwhelming folly.

As a solitary, never-to-be-repeated exception to the rule, I had been grudgingly accepted, if never approved. But I was hardly the only woman in Angland to be born with a gift and potential for magic. Those other girls, along with their descendants, deserved every chance that I had recklessly thrown away when I'd risked too much in my own experimentation.

At the time, I'd imagined my goal worth any danger: to prove my power beyond debate to everyone who flatly refused to work with a woman magician. Now, I finally understood the truth: the only way to change those attitudes for good was to use all of my hard-won skills and knowledge to train a whole new generation of magical girls as my successors. But with the entirety of the political and magical establishments of our nation irate and poised against my challenge...

Nothing could be allowed to go wrong.

"When exactly is the Boudiccate's inspection due to begin?" I asked Amy. "If we can take a few weeks to settle everyone in first—"

Amy held out the letter, grimacing. "They'll be with us within the next few hours, I expect."

"They're trying to ensure that we fail." I closed my eyes for one brief moment, gathering my scattered thoughts before they could break loose and send me raging.

So much for all of my extra preparations!

Really, there was only one consolation to be found: if the Boudiccate's inspectors arrived at the same time as my new students and all the bustle of their assorted baggage and anxious parents, I would hardly have any energy spare to yearn for my missing husband anymore, or to fret over those poisonous dreams that persisted in plaguing me.

I can do this, no matter what they think, I told myself firmly. *This time, I will not let myself fail.*

For the sake of my loyal, loving sister-in-law, who had risked so much to support me in this venture...

For the sake of all those brilliant, talented girls whom the Great Library stubbornly refused to train...

And yes, for my own sake, too, because—despite everything I had feared after the loss of my magic, and despite the haunting whispers of those dreams—I was neither helpless nor broken after all.

...And if anyone from the Boudiccate insulted Amy on this visit, I would simply have to murder them. That was all.

At the other end of the house, the great bell sounded, vibrating through the walls.

I lifted my chin, suppressing the panic that wanted to choke me, and I gave my sister-in-law my most confident smile. "Well, then," I said, "let us go and welcome our first arrivals to Thornfell College of Magic."

2

Six months ago, Thornfell had been nothing more than my family's ancestral dower house: rambling, ivy-choked, absurdly over-large for its intended purpose, and almost entirely unused. It had been designed to be a safe haven for the men of my family to retire to once their wives passed away and their daughters (or more dangerously, daughters-in-law) assumed full control of Harwood House.

Between tragic accidents and loving family relations, though, it had been over a century since it had been used as anything but dusty storage space for the most unbearable wedding gifts, the most outmoded furniture, and the most baffling but indisposable family heirlooms—such as twelve closely handwritten volumes of observations on the plant life of the Harwood estate, composed by my most eccentric ancestor, the infamous recluse Romulus Harwood, before his tragically early death. The family had apparently discovered those volumes in his room, collectively shrugged, and shelved them in Thornfell's abandoned library to molder in dignity well out of sight, along with all the books of magic too antiquated to be kept any longer at Harwood House.

In fact, over the twenty-eight years of my own life, as the wild woodlands beyond had gradually invaded Thornfell's overgrown gardens—exploratory roots and branches stretching closer to its red brick walls every year—the house had been very nearly forgotten even by our own family. When I'd first moved here from the bright elegance and comfort of Harwood House in preparation for my wedding —only to find myself left alone when Wrexham was abruptly summoned away—I'd felt quite horribly cut off from the vibrancy of my own family home.

Now, though, as Amy and I walked through the maze of interlocking rooms that led from the refurbished library of magic to the front entryway, I looked with deep satisfaction at the warm, modern fey-lights that lined the freshly wallpapered walls. Amy and I had decorated it all together, with Jonathan's help in researching historical details that would add richness and personality to the ambience. Now, the whole house was patterned in shades of bronze, gold, copper, and green with the leaping stags, ravens, and boars that had each symbolized different aspects of my family's magical heritage at various points over the centuries. The effect was remarkably handsome, comfortable, and welcoming, and I could hardly have imagined it a few months ago.

Of course, my magician-ancestors would have had a collective fit of the vapors at my radical transformation of this masculine retreat. My own late father had done everything he could to quash my unladylike fascination with magic, whilst he'd struggled in vain to instill it in Jonathan. Still, there was no opening for the Boudiccate's representatives to find any fault in the house's transformation. Thornfell had been as radically reborn as I had in the past several months, both of us reimagining ourselves toward a common purpose, and I gave the wall of the final reception room a reassuring stroke as I passed.

No matter which great challenge we were about to meet, Thornfell and I would welcome it together. Whether it was an irate politician hoping to shut us down, an anxious parent in need of calm reassurance, or...

"*No food set out to await me*?" An unexpected—and horrifying—male voice rose in outrage in the foyer ahead. "D'you mean to say I've rattled halfway across the country to this ramshackle little hidey-hole only to be *starved* when I finally arrive? Do you *know* who you're talking to, woman?"

Oh, no. My jaw dropped open. I turned to stare at Amy in disbelief.

"Is that...?" she began, her own eyes wide.

"It is," I said in utter disgust, "*Gregory Luton*."

Young Luton was the most widely-loathed weather wizard in Angland...for good reason. Amy and I had met him at a Winter Solstice house party months ago, but I had hoped never to renew our acquaintance.

"What can *he* be doing here?" I muttered. "It's not as if he needs any more education." After all, he had always claimed—loudly—to be the best weather wizard to have ever graduated from the Great Library of Trinivantium. It was the only reason he'd been allowed back into their hallowed halls long enough to attain his degree, after getting himself expelled in his first year for insulting all of his professors. "Of all the worst days for him to come and stick his nose in..."

Amy frowned, cocking her head. "Who is it that he's speaking to? I can't quite hear—"

"Oh, *no*!" I scooped up my skirts and ran the last several feet of the corridor, abandoning all the dignity to be expected of a headmistress. Some catastrophes were too horrifying to face with composure—and when I burst into the foyer a moment later, I realized that I had arrived just in time.

Thick golden hair fluttered with romantic abandon around Gregory Luton's handsome, petulant face. Clad head to toe in peacock blue and green, the self-described greatest weather wizard in Angland was heaving a heavy valise in his hand, only too clearly preparing to throw it at my most valued—and most dangerous—servant.

"Mr. Luton!" I barked, pointing one minatory finger.

A year ago, I would have cast a spell to freeze him. But my politician mother had never required magic in order to work *her* will upon the world—and I withered him now with exactly the same glare that the famous Miranda Harwood had used to cow far more powerful mages than him. "Drop. the. valise. *Now!*" I ordered.

Rolling his blue eyes, Luton gave a heavy sigh and dropped the valise to the wooden floor with a thud. From the sound of its impact, he must have packed at least a dozen books along with his questionable finery. I had no idea why he'd brought it with him for this uninvited social call, but I couldn't summon up the energy to care.

I had far more urgent matters to attend to. Without a second look at my unwanted visitor, I turned to my new housekeeper, whom I'd only managed to attract in the first place with an astonishingly high wage and intensely sincere compliments. "Miss Birch." I gulped hard as I took in the pursed fury on her wizened face, and the way her long, bony fingers rapped against her thin, crossed arms. "Miss Birch, I do hope—that is to say, I regret any—"

"Insults!" she snapped. "In *my own house!*"

Surely she wouldn't call it *her* house if she was planning

to abandon it in disgust? I flung a frantic look at my sister-in-law, who had arrived at a more sedate pace behind me.

"My dear Miss Birch." Amy crossed the foyer in a few graceful steps, beaming. "How good of you to help Cassandra greet our new arrivals today. You've worked miracles here in the last week! Thornfell has never looked so welcoming before."

"Hmmph." Miss Birch glowered, her hazel eyes half-slitted and gleaming like a cat's. Wild magic skittered through the air, sending goosebumps shivering across my skin. Even the self-absorbed Luton jerked his head up in surprise.

"What was that?" he asked sharply.

I stepped quickly between him and Miss Birch. "Amy was just reminiscing yesterday," I said, "about those scones you gave us last week. She said she'd never tasted anything like them. Didn't you, Amy?"

Amy didn't even blink at the non-sequitur. "Of course! I would never wish to steal your baking secrets, Miss Birch, but *would* it be possible to steal just one more of your delicious treats for myself at some point today?"

Miss Birch's scowl softened, as scowls so often did around my sister-in-law. "Well," she said, "for someone who truly *appreciates* my work, I suppose I might be able to find one spare from the collection I just took out from the oven. But if I'm expected to *fetch and carry* for some—"

"Absolutely not!" I said firmly, and rose to my tiptoes to block whatever Luton's own expression might be. "Mr. Luton has clearly lost his way. You won't be required to help him with anything else here ever again."

"Hmmph," repeated Miss Birch, and stalked out of the room with Amy hurrying after her.

Phew. I let out my breath and sank back down onto the

soles of my slippered feet as the sounds of Amy's soothing small-talk floated through the air like the calming scent of lavender. *One crisis averted.*

The crisis who still lounged carelessly in my own front hall, though, let out a disbelieving laugh that made my spine clench. "And I'd thought my aunt's servants were useless! I know we're trapped out in the back of beyond, but—"

Seething, I swung around. "I would *not*," I said, "make the mistake of disrespecting—or underestimating—Miss Birch."

"You want me to bow down to a housekeeper?" He snorted. "You may be trying to turn the whole world topsy-turvy right now, but all the same—"

"Miss Birch," I said, "is a highly valued member of my staff."

I ended my explanation there, raising my eyebrows in challenge. I had no intention of sharing other people's confidences, even less interest in sharing my private reasoning with young Luton—and I would never allow him or anyone else to treat a member of my staff badly.

But it had been basic human kindness to issue him a particular warning when it came to Miss Birch—because of course, I hadn't hired her *only* for her remarkable house-keeping abilities.

"Ha!" said Luton. "I'm a member of your staff, too, don't forget, and I would have imagined I'd rate *rather* higher than—"

"*What*?" My jaw dropped. "You're a—what?"

"And everyone *claims* women are the more practical sex..." He heaved a weary sigh. "Don't you even recall requesting that I be hired?"

"I did no such thing!" I'd hired every member of Thornfell's staff myself, and they were already on-site, too, all except...

Oh, no. I shut my eyes against the horror of the most obvious explanation.

My new professor of weather wizardry *hadn't* yet arrived —and weather wizardry was the one area of magical specialty that I couldn't teach my students myself, in a pinch. It was taught in an entirely separate curriculum at the Great Library, and I'd never cared to look into it on my own. Unfortunately, as I'd found to my dismay over the last few months, even the most eccentric and impoverished weather wizards in all of Angland had refused every blandishment I'd offered to recruit them, because the Great Library had issued a blanket mandate: no graduate was to *ever* take up any position at my school, on pain of having their names struck forever from the legendary register of alumni.

That was why I was covering every other aspect of magical training at the school myself—and why Wrexham had taken up the added task of hunting out an available weather wizard during all of his missions across the nation in the past five weeks. In his last, scrawled note, which had appeared on my mantelpiece only two days earlier, he had assured me that he'd finally secured a clever, well-qualified weather wizard willing to anger the Great Library by taking up an appointment at my school. He had neglected to mention that wizard's name in his note, and I'd been far too relieved to care about that small detail.

Now I knew why my darling husband had been so uncharacteristically 'forgetful.'

"Mrs. Wrexham," said Luton, "I don't know if you're aware, but you are making the most unnerving noise in your throat right now. I find it deeply irritating."

"I was just...anticipating my next conversation with my husband." As I flicked my eyes open, I bared my teeth in the semblance of a smile. "He and I have a great deal to discuss, it seems. And for future reference, I am still Miss Harwood."

Had I been a politician, as my parents had intended, Wrexham would have automatically taken my surname upon our marriage; but I'd passed the mantle of my mother's political inheritance on to Amy with deep relief, and she'd taken the title of 'Mrs. Harwood' upon her own marriage instead.

In another kind of marriage, with a magician as the husband and an ordinary, nonpolitical sort of woman as the wife, I would indeed have become Mrs. Wrexham, as Luton had so annoyingly presumed.

But Wrexham and I were a new kind of match—the first known marriage in Anglish history between two magicians of different genders. So, in the end, we'd followed the practice of those couples who shared a gender rather than a profession, and we'd each retained our own surnames after all.

It might have seemed a radical decision to anyone else, but Mr. Luton looked ready to perish from the tedium of being forced to consider anyone else's circumstances for a single moment. "I *am* carrying a letter for you," he sighed, "but I'd much rather have a cup of tea or claret before we have to suffer through all of that nonsense about salaries and exactly how you'll manage all of my requirements. What on earth possessed you to build a school so far from civilization?"

"Argh!" In a last-ditch moment of hope, I strode forward and yanked the front door open to peer outside, just in case...but the hired carriage that had brought him had already disappeared down the long curve of the drive that led first to Harwood House, my family's ancient home, and from thence onward to the wide world beyond.

There was to be no easy disposal of my newest member of staff after all...and worst of all, I had to admit that Wrexham had been right: if I meant to prove to the Boudiccate that I was offering my students a comprehensive education, one that could stand proudly in comparison to the Great Library's syllabus, then even hiring Luton was better than hiring no weather wizard at all.

It was a bitter pill to swallow...and the thought of Miss Birch's expression, when I had to inform her that he would be staying after all, was even more intimidating.

I let the front door fall shut with a thud. "For once, Mr. Luton, I agree with you." I sighed. "I could do with a great deal more tea before you utter another word."

3

A quarter of an hour later, I was resting limply in a wingback chair in the staff parlor with my latest cup of tea propped between my hands as young Luton's extraordinary demands and absurdly over-inflated expectations washed across me in an endless cascade.

When the bell at the door suddenly broke through his monologue, I leaped to my feet so quickly that a tidal wave of tea splashed from my porcelain cup into its saucer.

Salvation!

If the Boudiccate's haughtiest inspectors, in their worst possible moods, could only stalk in right now to save me from my newest staff member, I would overwhelm them with the sincerity of my welcome.

"Alas!" I placed the sloshing, over-full saucer onto a side table and briskly wiped my hands. "I must attend to our new arrivals, but I'm certain you can find your own way to your staff cottage, Mr. Luton. It's past the stables and the gardens, just before the woodland begins behind Thornfell, and—"

"I beg your pardon." He snorted, not bothering to lower his own cup of tea as he sprawled back in his chair. "If you'll recall, Miss Harwood, you still haven't even heard all of my terms or—"

"*Mister* Luton." Crossing my arms, I gave him my best glower. "This little chat has been an...*enlightening* introduction to your tenure here at Thornfell, but you know as well as I that you are in desperate need of this position. Therefore, you are in no position to make a single one of these demands upon me."

His jaw dropped open, but I held up one hand to halt any outraged—and outrageous—protests. "I was at the same Winter Solstice house party as your aunt, you may recall. I overheard her informing all of the ladies there *exactly* how impossible you've found it to secure any paying work since graduation, no matter how many times she's called in favors from her oldest friends. Despite all of her influence and your own undeniable gifts, the reputation you left behind at the Great Library has left you entirely unhireable."

A wave of red swept upwards from young Luton's collar. "I was the finest weather mage to study at the Great Library in decades! If you could see the marks that I achieved—"

"Those were *academic* achievements," I said flatly. "As we both know by now, the realities of life outside the Library are rather different." A wave of reluctant fellow-feeling swept through me as his jaw tightened and his gaze fell away from mine. "You know," I continued in a softer tone, "I couldn't persuade anyone to hire me for mage-work, either, despite all of my own achievements at the Great Library. Of course, in my case, it was for a different reason, but—"

"Well, clearly." He gave a snort of amusement, the color fading from his fair skin. "Who would wish to hire a *woman* to cast their magic?"

Clenching my jaw, I took a deep, sustaining breath. "Regardless. You've been granted your chance at long last,

Mr. Luton, to prove that you *can* shine outside the Great Library after all. If I were you, I wouldn't waste it...and I certainly wouldn't make any more foolish comments like that last one if you ever hope to prove yourself a useful teacher to our students. They deserve your respect, and you *will* give it to them.

"Oh, and..." I was halfway through the doorway when I remembered my final obligation and turned back. "There are several lovely pathways to explore the woods just past your cottage, but you shouldn't venture down any of them for at least another month or so." At his baffled frown, I added: "It's bluebell season, you see."

"Pfft." He hunched one shoulder, scowling down into his teacup. "What piffle."

"Piffle?" I raised my eyebrows. "I don't know where you spent *your* childhood, but I can tell you from experience that the fey take a keen interest in these parts at this time of year—and my family agreed a long time ago to leave their woods in peace in bluebell season. If we don't bother them, they won't bother us—so take care *not* to venture inside the woods yet, if you please, and make certain you don't let any of our students wander in that direction, either."

There. I'd done my duty. With a sigh of relief, I shut the door on his petulant scowl and hurried down the corridor to greet my next arrivals.

The great bell rang again and again as the next few hours compressed into a happy blur of activity. A growing collection of young women strode through Thornfell's refurbished doors, slapping their gloves against their sides and glowing with excitement and nervous energy, whilst their commanding mothers swept in after them to ask final, probing questions and inspect all of their bedrooms for any last-minute threats.

Amy and I plied the mothers with Miss Birch's finest scones as the daughters settled into their living quarters. I answered every challenging technical question, while Amy supplied all of the soothing charm. Even my infant niece—once my brother had delivered her for her regular afternoon feed—supplied a perfectly charming distraction for all of us. Energetic young voices echoed up and down the corridors for the first time in Thornfell's history.

One day, I hoped, I would standardize the entrance age for Thornfell College of Magic as the Great Library had done centuries ago. This initial class of students ranged from seventeen to nearly twenty-three years of age, a disparity I'd worried over more than once. Still, I'd been in no position to be exacting when so few hardheaded Anglish mothers would allow their precious heirs such a scandalous education in the first place—and I could hardly punish any talented young woman for the year of her birth. I knew too well what it was to hunger for magic and be denied it.

It was an ache under my own skin every day.

One of the latest arrivals was one of the oldest—and the only one of my students with whom I was already acquainted. "Miss Banks!" Smiling, I rose from the round table where I'd sat with Amy and three stern, icy matriarchs who were helplessly thawing as they gathered around my niece. Leaving them in Amy's capable hands—with Jonathan hovering nearby, ready to leap into the breach should baby Miranda set up any sudden storms—I hurried across the parlor to clasp Miss Banks's small white hands. "Was your journey tolerable?"

Beaming, Miss Banks nodded, her fair ringlets rippling around her face. "I spent most of it reading. I've read *every* book you sent me. I read the Larchmont twice in a row! And then I studied it again on the journey here. I feel *so* close to understanding the formulas. If I could only—"

"We'll practice them here," I promised. "Of course, you'll have to wait for the rest of your classmates to catch up with you, but we should reach those spells by October at the latest."

Her face fell, and I laughed, giving her hands a sympathetic squeeze. "Who knows? Perhaps we'll find time to study them individually beforehand. Then you could help me tutor the others later on."

"I'd like that." There was a glint of determination in her forget-me-not blue eyes, matching the willpower I'd learned to respect in our acquaintance thus far.

Miss Banks might be soft-spoken, small, and deceptively pliable-looking, but she was the secret fiancée of one of the Boudiccate's greatest political hopes for this next generation. Together, those two young women had hatched a radical plan long before I'd met them, a plan that would launch both of them into the public eye within the next decade—and Miss Banks, I noted, was the only one of my students to have traveled across the country entirely on her own, without exhibiting any concern about the matter.

She would need every bit of that hidden steel to carry her through the controversies to come. I gave her an approving nod in return as I stepped back.

"Now," I said, turning to the room at large, "I believe everyone has arrived, so—"

Before I could finish my sentence, a whirlwind exploded in the center of the room. The air blurred before me. Wind whipped in a tightly controlled circle around the gradually solidifying outlines of four people...and my jaw dropped at the outrageous extravagance of the gesture.

Our Boudiccate inspectors were making their arrival

into a statement—with a stunningly wasteful misuse of magical power. There was no sensible reason they couldn't have simply arrived by carriage; no reason *at all* except to make a declaration of dominance in *my* new school's parlor. The task of transporting another person required a phenomenal output of magic. To transport more than one was nearly unheard-of—and to do it with such astonishing accuracy was positively miraculous.

Whatever officer of magic had been required to take on this absurd task would be depleted for days, if not weeks, afterward—and among all the clever officers of magic for the Boudiccate, I only knew a few gentlemen with the power and skill to judge a pinpoint landing across the country with more than one passenger in their wake.

Only a few...

My heartbeat thrummed in my throat and wrists as I started forward, my mouth dry and my skin alight. It had been so many weeks, so many endless nights—

The air cleared, and I rocked to a halt.

It wasn't Wrexham. I should have known better than to hope, even for an instant, that it could be.

The gentleman who stood with his back to me now had tight salt-and-pepper curls above the sliver of dark brown skin displayed over his elegant cravat, and I recognized him immediately. Lionel Westgate had been chief magical officer for the Boudiccate ever since the days when I'd been a sulky young girl dragged by my mother to observe her political meetings against my will.

She had butted heads more than once with Mr. Westgate —a powerful magician and an honorable man with a will more inflexible than iron and a mind that was never easily changed nor diverted. Like my mother, I had always respected him, even when he had infuriated me in later years for his obdurate refusal to even consider opening his brotherhood of magical officers to me as a female recruit.

In that, at least, he was no more nor less hidebound than most gentlemen in Angland. *My* husband was not so stupidly closed-minded...but we could have done a great deal worse in the Boudiccate's choice of magical officer to accompany this aggravating inspection. So, I swallowed down my irrational disappointment as I looked beyond Mr. Westgate to see who our political judges would be.

Three women stood before him, and the first was nearly fully blocked from view by his broad shoulders, but as I recognized the other two, my lips stretched wide into a smile of pure, astonished wonder.

Lady Cosgrave, stylish as always in a peacock-feathered bonnet and a silver-trimmed pelisse, was one of the youngest members of the Boudiccate, still only in her mid-forties. More importantly, she'd been one of Amy's closest friends for years. To win her as one of our auditors was a gift beyond any I'd dared to hope for—but behind her stood an even more welcome sight: Lady Cosgrave's young, long-limbed blonde cousin—and political protégée—Miss Fennell, who was my own Miss Banks's secret fiancée.

There was no politician in the world who could be more committed to the success of our radical new school...because tradition dictated that no lady should be invited to enter the Boudiccate unless she was married to a practicing magician. Until now, that ancient rule had prevented any ambitious young politician from wedding another lady, no matter what her own private inclinations might be—so for the sake of Miss Fennell's romantic and political future, Thornfell College of Magic *could not* be allowed to close down.

My shoulders relaxed for the first time in weeks as I

swept forward without waiting for Amy to lead the ceremonies as usual. "Lady Cosgrave!" I held out my hand. "Miss Fennell! *And* Mr. Westgate. *What* a pleasure to welcome—"

"Miss Harwood." Lady Cosgrave cut me off with a tone more chilling than ice. "And...Mrs. Harwood. Of course." She flashed a quick, cool glance at Amy and then looked away, dismissing my sister-in-law entirely. She didn't grant my brother—whom she'd known for twenty years—so much as a look.

Frowning, I let my hand fall to my side, unclasped. Beside Lady Cosgrave, Miss Fennell's strong face was set in inscrutable lines...and her hazel gaze was fixed as firmly upon *my* face as if her own fiancée—whom she hadn't seen in weeks—wasn't standing a scant five paces away from me.

Something was very, very wrong—and I knew it even before the third woman stepped out from Mr. Westgate's shadow.

"Well, well, well. Cassandra Harwood, how you've grown. Or should I say Cassandra *Wrexham* now?"

"It's Cassandra Harwood." My voice sounded odd to my own ears, my numb lips moving on no more than instinct...that, and my old refusal to ever let this woman see how deeply her words always stabbed into my bones.

I had been a woman grown for many years. But the sound of that too-familiar voice flung me directly back into the lowest point of my adolescence, before Amy had taken on the role of my mother's assistant and slipped seamlessly into our family forever...

After Jonathan had walked quietly into our family's private drawing room one day to find our mother's then-assistant tormenting me in that soft, silky voice that Annabel Renwick had always used whenever she cornered me on her own, without anyone else close enough to over-hear us.

It had been as obvious to Annabel as it had been to me that I was unsuited to being my mother's heir. I had never disagreed with her on *that*. But the particular zeal with which she, at nineteen years of age, had chosen to mali-ciously attack a twelve-year-old girl for that simple accident of birth—for months on end!—was enough to stun me in retrospect.

I'd been far too proud to ever tell my mother about that stream of sly, vicious commentary—a lurking threat that came to cling like poisonous vines around my days, a constantly watching menace in my own home. Likewise, I'd refused to sensibly go into hiding in my bedroom, no matter how unsafe every other room in our house had become. Thus, it had taken months before any adult could step in and help me escape from her.

"Still," Annabel said now, a smile playing on her generous lips, "I suppose I shouldn't be surprised at the chaos you've caused for our entire nation. You always *were* the worst student of politics I ever met."

"Luckily," said Amy, "she was one of the best students of magic ever to attend the Great Library." Sweeping to my side, she took my arm in hers and looked expectantly at the Boudiccate's chief officer of Magic. "Isn't that right, Mr. Westgate?"

My tight chest eased just enough to let me finally release my breath. Amy had chosen her target and her question well, as always—for as much as Lionel Westgate might disapprove of me and my endeavor, he would never deign to lie in public.

"Yes." He gave a tight nod.

A ripple of pleasure passed through the audience of my

students' mothers, and recalled me to the moment. Too many eyes were watching for me to allow myself to be paralyzed by shock—or to let my emotions rip free into long-repressed fury.

I was no awkward twelve-year-old girl anymore being forced into a shape she could never fit. I was an acknowledged expert in the field that I loved, and I was creating my own space in the world, no matter what a venomous adder like Annabel Renwick might think of it. If I hadn't been so stupidly proud all those years ago, I would have let Jonathan tell Mother the truth about her assistant when he'd first discovered it. Instead, on my desperate insistence, he had created a fictional lesser offense that had got her safely dismissed from Mother's service—but had allowed her to keep her entrée in the political world.

That was a mistake that more than one member of our family had paid for across the years. If Amy could bring herself now to face down the woman who'd stolen her own promised seat in the Boudiccate all those years ago, I could do no less than stand tall by her side.

I closed my free hand over Amy's where it rested on my arm, and I straightened my shoulders. "I can see that this inspection will be a...fascinating experience for all of us," I said. "Welcome to Thornfell College of Magic. I do hope you'll all make yourselves quite at home."

There was no chance left at a fair inspection. Annabel had blamed me for her dismissal from my mother's side; she had been deceptive and malicious for as long as I'd known her; and I had no doubts of what decision had already been made for Thornfell's fate at the end of this week.

However, I did have one burning certainty to support me as I smiled fiercely at my old tormentor.

She should have accepted her good fortune, all those

years ago, when I'd foolishly allowed her to escape my mother's wrath. Miranda Harwood might have been a demanding—and sometimes impossible—mother, but she had been a lioness in defending her children against all enemies. She would have been utterly ruthless in the destruction of Annabel's prospects if she'd known the torment I'd endured...

But *I* was my mother's daughter, and I had a whole school full of hopeful young women to protect now.

Annabel Renwick had no idea of the battle she was in for.

᪥ 4 ᪥

By the end of the evening, a dull, throbbing ache emanated from my jaw, which had been clenched beyond womanly endurance for hours. But I'd won my first skirmish: I hadn't risen to a single one of Annabel's taunts, no matter how enticingly she'd dangled them before me. Better yet, even the harshest judge could have found no real fault in the opening lecture I'd just delivered to my new students at the end of their delicious evening meal.

Young Luton, of course, had spent most of that lecture making faces of skeptical consideration throughout even my mildest points as he sat at the back of the room, scoffing an entire bowl-full of Miss Birch's candied almonds after delivering his own introductory remarks to our new students; but the fact that he made no audible comments of disagreement was a clear sign that he too was making an attempt at self-control.

The most qualified judge in the room sat in the chair beside Mr. Luton, listening with no expression at all on his lean, dark face—except for one brief wince when Luton spat a whole shower of almond fragments onto his lap in a choking fit near the end, just after I'd described exactly how weather wizardry would fit into our syllabus.

Unlike young Luton, Lionel Westgate was not prone to giving away his private thoughts. But he rose as I strode towards the door, following the exodus of chattering young magicians on their way to bed, and his pose was watchful enough to make me pause.

"Mr. Westgate." I glanced beyond him to the cluster of Boudiccate inspectors, all huddled together in one corner of the room, murmuring too quietly to be overheard. "Am I being summoned to an official meeting?"

"No." His voice grave, he gestured discreetly toward the door. "May I beg the favor of a tour around the grounds before you retire for the evening, Miss Harwood?"

My head felt light and brittle with exhaustion. I had been pushing myself through the day on nervous energy, and I was rapidly running out of that finite resource. I still had to find an opportunity to consult with Miss Banks and Miss Fennell before either of them went to bed, and I needed to carefully re-think my lesson plans for tomorrow, now that they would be given under Boudiccate inspection.

But Lionel Westgate was my husband's supervisor and one of the most highly respected magicians in all Angland. It would be madness to turn down any opportunity to argue my case with him in private.

"Of course." I drew a deep, invigorating breath.

Fresh air, I told myself firmly. All I needed was the taste of the cool night air to start my thoughts moving briskly again.

I'd worked through sleepless nights often enough in my student days—but then, of course, I'd had Wrexham working beside me at the same ancient study table in the Great Library, the two of us staying awake together long after all of our fellow students had given up and gone to bed. We'd teased and challenged each other to ever greater heights in our endless rivalry to win the highest marks, the greatest victories...and most of all, to impress each other at every turn.

Those nights, I hadn't needed any sleep; I'd felt utterly *alive* for the first time in my life. We hadn't so much as kissed, at first—we'd barely even touched except for accidental brushes of arms and shoulders that had left me tingling for hours afterward. The mere, crackling awareness of all that lean, focused brilliance at my side, like captured flame—his silky, smooth dark hair tumbling over his forehead as he'd leaned over his books; his long, light brown fingers turning the pages and inspiring dizzying fantasies of how they'd feel if they ever brushed against my skin—had been more than enough to keep me pricklingly wide awake and determined to prove myself to both of us, no matter what that took.

And now, the memory of those late nights in the Great Library was enough to turn my smile genuine as I led the chief magical officer of the Boudiccate through the bronze-and-green corridors of my own school, past scattered girls who'd lingered in the wide foyer to chat on their way back to their private quarters.

They shot us awed and wide-eyed glances; I gave them firm nods in return. "Don't stay up too late," I told them. "Classes start early in the morning, and you'll want to be alert."

For the first time in all the years I'd known him, Mr. Westgate's stern lips twitched in unmistakable amusement. He had the grace to stay silent until the great front door swung shut behind us, leaving us alone and unobserved except by the birds and small insects who swooped through the cool, darkening air and pecked at the pebbled drive beyond our feet.

With all the loud and bustling confusion of student arrivals at an end, the wild denizens of the fields and woods around Thornfell were re-emerging to claim their territory for the night. It had always been a favorite time of mine to sit outside and think in peace. If I knew my brother and my sister-in-law, they would be outside right now, too, taking their usual evening walk around the lake that glimmered in the distance, beyond the great bulk of Harwood House.

Mr. Westgate inquired, "Did you often retire early to bed in your own student days, Miss Harwood?"

I aimed him a sidelong glance, my smile turning mischievous. "Did *you*?"

At that, he let out a huff of air that might almost have been a laugh, and turned to cast his own sharp gaze across the rolling landscape.

"Of course, you already know the Aelfen Mere," I said, gesturing toward the lake in the distance.

Along with the Boudiccate's other magical officers, he'd attended annual balls beneath those waves in my younger years, back when my mother was still one of the Boudiccate's most famous hostesses and my late father's greatest spell had still held sway beneath the lake. To begin our tour of the rest of the estate now, I led him in a circling path around Thornfell's rambling red brick walls.

Rabbits, small and brown and quick, startled out of the grass before us as we walked, and a flash of red in the corner of my eye heralded a fox slipping swiftly out of sight. The woods rustled temptingly beyond our modest gardens, thick and green and far more vibrant than any of the plain hedges my new gardener had tamed into submission a few weeks ago. We were lucky, at least, to be at the height of spring; after a few discreet evening visits from Miss Birch across the past week or two, I could already glimpse bright flowers starting to unfurl in their new beds, where thick, tangled undergrowth had reigned supreme for the past twenty years or more.

Still, I wasn't surprised to see Mr. Westgate's gaze slip past the unimpressive gardens—and young Luton's plain stone cottage—to the great, whispering woods that sprawled beyond, large enough to swallow Thornfell's grounds many times over.

"Your father used to tell stories about those woods," he said. "He claimed they were some of the most magical in Angland."

"They certainly are," I agreed, "but I wouldn't venture inside them while you're here. The—"

"Bluebell season, yes, yes, I know." He waved my words aside with one flick of his hand. "We all heard your warning after supper. *Both* warnings, in fact. I may be aging, Miss Harwood, but you may rest assured that my ears still function perfectly well."

I bit back a sigh. "I wouldn't doubt it, but I thought I'd better repeat it more than once tonight. Students have never been famous for taking heed of sensible warnings."

"Hmm." He gave a quiet snort and shook his head, clasping his hands behind his back. "You never did, as I recall—before *or* after your student days."

Well. There were so many ways to interpret that statement that I couldn't even begin to respond. From the first time I'd revealed my own magical powers to the world at large, defying all of my mother's threats and warnings, to the moment last year when I had cast a spell that everyone *knew* no solitary magician could ever manage, in my final attempt to prove myself to everyone who refused to hire a woman to cast magic...

I took a deep, steadying breath. "We all make mistakes," I said. "But with luck, we can learn from them—and help others to learn, too."

"An admirable way of putting it." He turned his fierce gaze to me, his thick brows lowered. "But how many other people should pay the price for our mistakes?"

My throat felt suddenly dry. "I beg your pardon?"

"All the times I've visited this estate..." He shook his head slowly, his gaze never leaving mine. "*So* famously magical, so undeniably glittering...yes, you Harwoods have always shone in politics and magic alike. There's no question of the power in your family. But perhaps that's what's led to your fatal flaw: as a dynasty, you were gifted too much *power* to care for unexciting *duty*."

A sharp spike of pain jabbed through my jaw as it re-clenched. I had to force myself to breathe steadily, in and out through my teeth, as memories jostled before my eyes— my mother working so tirelessly through her too-short life, throwing everything she had at the good of the nation; Jonathan, supporting all of us throughout with his quiet, thoughtful kindness and his deeply principled strength; and Amy, who cared so fiercely for *everyone*...

It took a long moment before I could allow myself to speak. "My family," I said, "has raised every generation for *centuries* to serve Angland to the utmost of our abilities. We—"

"The *utmost of your abilities*," he repeated. "An exhila-rating challenge, to be sure. But what happens when the good of the nation demands that you relinquish your own abilities? That you step aside from personal glory for Angland's sake?"

And now we came to that same bitter old question, still furiously unresolved, all these years after I'd first won my place in the Great Library and naïvely thought the matter decided forever. My teeth ground together and my eyes narrowed as I glared up into his pitiless face. "It can *never* be for the good of the nation for half of Angland's natural magic-workers to be stifled in their abilities! If we *want* ours to be the strongest nation in the world, with a magical defense that none can match—"

"Cassandra Harwood," said Lionel Westgate with weary finality, "I've known you since you were a little girl. I watched your first public performance of magic beneath that lake, and I know as well as you that it had *nothing* to do with bolstering Angland's magical defenses. No, you only wished to show the extent of your own power off to the world—as you Harwoods are always *so* eager to do. Why do you think I never hired you as an officer of magic, despite all of your famous skills?"

The words landed like a physical blow; I had to clench every muscle to hold back a flinch. "This is not about me," I said through a tight throat. "It's about every magical young woman in Angland who deserves—"

"What of your own sister-in-law?" he inquired. "What does *she* deserve? Oh, she's a clever politician, everyone agrees on that. She could have become a member of the Boudiccate years ago. But your brother's insistence on following his personal passion for history rather than studying magic, as *his* duty required, kept her from achieving her own dreams. Now, she's lost her career entirely—because *you* couldn't bring yourself to admit that you had failed to prove a woman could be a magician after all."

His words struck hard at my rawest wounds. Still, I held

his gaze with a physical effort. "Amy chose to marry Jonathan, knowing full well that he would never be a magician. *He* didn't take away any of her dreams." That much, I knew for certain. I'd never met any couple more shiningly content in each other's company.

"Perhaps," said Mr. Westgate skeptically. "But you? You must have known how precarious her political position would become when you announced the creation of this scandalous establishment. Did you even think of what would happen to her?"

No. Curse it, I hadn't. I'd been far too focused on my own bright goal to see any details beyond it. But... "I told Amy she could denounce my school to save herself."

"But your own husband had no such option, did he?"

"*What*?" I took a quick step forward, my breath accelerating. "What are you talking about? What's happened to Wrexham?"

It had only been five weeks since I'd seen him; surely, *surely*, he would have told me in one of his letters if anything dreadful had occurred! He'd mentioned nixies and marsh-spirits and obstreperous farmers, but he'd certainly never mentioned any injuries. If he'd been hurt, and I didn't even know—!

"Even you," said Mr. Westgate with withering disdain, "must have noticed what the Boudiccate has been doing to him of late. Do you think he's always been flung about the countryside with never a moment to stop and rest? Or that any other officer in Angland is given *no* days off, for weeks in a row?"

"*Obviously*," I said through gritted teeth, "they're keeping us apart. But—"

"Oh, it's far more than that." The light in Mr. Westgate's eyes was pure fury. "As the man who has supervised every officer of magic for the past *twenty years*, I can tell you that they are intentionally driving him to resign. *Rajaram Wrexham!* One of the most brilliant, most astonishing magicians I've ever worked with—you must know he was meant to be my second-in-command within the next few years. He *should* be my replacement not long after that, and one of the most admired magicians in our country! But because of *your* selfish and reckless decisions—your *continued* recklessness beyond belief, even after all this time and all the lessons that any sensible woman would have learned by now!—the Boudiccate is treating him as so much rubbish to be discarded by the wayside.

"*That* is why I asked for this private word with you: to give you one final chance, here and now—if you have any real affection or respect for your own husband—to give up this mad endeavor for good. Only *think* of who will pay the price for your folly this time! If you go, tonight, to the visiting members of the Boudiccate—if you swear to them that you truly regret founding this school, and you agree to abandon it now, quietly, before any more damage is done..."

He gave a heavy sigh, and his strong shoulders slumped. "Well. I won't say that it would necessarily save his chances at the heights to which he *should* have risen. But it might at least save his career."

"...And shatter mine forever." My voice shook uncontrollably; my hands knotted into fists as emotions swirled within my chest.

Of *course* they were trying to push Wrexham into giving up his post in defeat. How could I not have seen it until now? But then—the truth was bitterly inescapable—Mr. Westgate had been right: I'd been so intent on my school and my own ambitions, I hadn't spared any time to consider

Wrexham's prospects. They'd always seemed far too sparkling to require any concern on my part.

All those years that he'd risen inexorably through the magical ranks of our nation whilst I'd languished, forgotten by the world at large, as every magical employer refused to hire me...

It had never even occurred to me that when I did finally carve out a place for myself, it would steal the space that Wrexham had earned.

My stomach twisted so hard, I nearly doubled over. But I was standing on Harwood ground—and whatever Lionel Westgate might think of us, *that* was a legacy I would not shame with weakness.

"My marriage is for myself and my husband to discuss," I said as icily as I could manage. "I'll bid you goodnight now, Mr. Westgate, and wish you a pleasant night's sleep."

His eyes narrowed into an outright glower. "And I suppose you'll sleep perfectly well yourself, even after everything I've said!"

"Undoubtedly." I couldn't stay a moment longer. I spun around to stalk back toward the house before my illusion of control could shatter entirely.

So much for consulting with Miss Banks and Miss Fennell before either of them went to bed! If I could only make it safely to my own room before releasing my tears of helpless fury, I would call it the highest of victories.

I had never been so thankful for Thornfell's unassuming back entrance, half-hidden by the ivy that grew over the small wooden door. It led to a narrow flight of stairs that allowed me to bypass every public room and stay safely hidden until I reached the level of my bedroom, a full storey above any of my students' quarters. I took the steps at a near-run, desperate to release my frantic emotions in any way that I could.

By the time I reached my doorway, I was panting, strands of hair slipping and sliding free from my chignon. I turned the handle and collapsed inside...

...To find warm fey-lights burning in the room and my husband sprawled loosely in the chair before my desk, his long legs crossed and his smile wry as he looked me up and down with one dark eyebrow raised.

"A good first day of work, then, Harwood?"

5

"Ohhh!"

He wasn't a dream or a fey-illusion. Wrexham was *here*, in the flesh, sitting *finally* in our bedroom where he belonged!

I lunged across the room before he could disappear again.

Those long legs of his had always moved quickly. By the time I collided with him, he was on his feet and ready. One arm slid possessively around my waist; his other hand curved around my head, fingers tangling in my hair. His warm lips met mine with the same fierce hunger that had driven me wild with longing for the past five weeks.

The last time we'd kissed had been just after our wedding, a kiss of frustration and farewell—but only, we'd hoped, for two or three days at the most. Now, five weeks later, his light brown cheeks were rough with prickly stubble. His shoulder-length black hair slid softly against my fingers.

I needed to touch every inch of him to prove that he was real.

His long fingers were already pulling out the pins that held up my hair in its proper headmistress's knot. I pulled back just far enough to shake out the last of them with a breathless laugh, letting them scatter to the floor as my hair fell down in a thick brown veil around my shoulders.

Finally.

"You're late." I measured his shoulders with my hands. "Our wedding night should have been five weeks ago. Remember?"

"It was worth the wait." Wrexham's voice was fervent. His gorgeous brown eyes dilated as his gaze swept across me. "If you had any idea how impatient I've been for this moment..."

"How impatient *you've* been?" Rolling my eyes, I pointed imperiously at the empty bed. "There. *Now*. Immediately, husband!"

He broke into a grin that left me helplessly dazzled. "As my wife commands." With a sudden lunge, Wrexham scooped me up into his arms and swept me across the room with him. We landed in a giddily breathless and laughing pile on the bed a moment later...and I rolled over to bury my face in his neck, wrapping my arms tightly around his chest, finally and exactly where I belonged.

"I've *missed* you," I whispered into his skin. It tasted of salt and of sweat and of *Wrexham*, unique and irreplaceable. My husband. My best friend in the world, all these years. The man I'd tried to give up for his own good when I had lost my magic—but who had never, ever given up on me in return.

The second half of my soul, from the moment we'd met.

...And, according to Lionel Westgate, the man whose life I had ruined through my own unforgivable self-absorption.

"What's amiss?" One hand gently stroked my hair; the

other slid across my back, pulling me even closer into Wrexham's embrace. "*Harwood.* What are you worrying over now? If you've remembered some vital work that needs to be done before you come to bed, I'll wait. You know I'll understand. Just—"

"*No.*" I bit out the word as frustration and guilt cascaded through me, burning deep underneath my skin.

There was no chance of me abandoning him when I'd finally got him back—but it was *exactly* the wrong moment to be reminded of my work.

"If you have any real affection or respect for your own husband..."

Wrexham had never argued against my school. From the first moment I'd envisioned it, he'd listened enthusiastically to every one of my plans and offered intelligent suggestions and unstinting support. He was *proud* of what I had achieved here—or at least, so I would have sworn, an hour earlier.

"Now, Harwood." He shifted beneath me, brushing aside the veil of hair between us and nudging gently at my downturned face. "You might as well come out with it. You know we don't keep secrets from one another anymore."

"Then why didn't *you* tell me?" The words blurted themselves out almost without my volition. Like a tortoise hiding from the truth, I kept my face buried in the safe hollow between his neck and his shoulder, his silky black hair pillowing my forehead as I awaited his reply.

"I...beg your pardon?" He let out a half-laugh of confusion, still stroking his fingers soothingly through my hair. "I'm afraid you'll have to be clearer than that, my love, because I haven't slept much for several weeks now. I've been longing for my wife, you see." He dropped a kiss on my head. "What exactly do you think I've been hiding from you? And when would I have even had the time?"

I sighed into his neck. "Mr. Westgate is here with the Boudiccate's inspectors. He told me *exactly* what's been happening to you because of me."

"...Ah." Wrexham's fingers stilled on my head in mid-stroke.

I pushed myself up onto my elbows, and he let me go, his hand slipping free from my hair. As I braced myself above him, frowning, I searched in vain for any clues in his aggravatingly neutral expression.

He had always been too good at hiding his thoughts. It had served him well over the years as one of those rare scholarship students who'd successfully won his way into the Great Library, but it made my whole body clench with frustration now. I could *feel* his agile brain working furiously behind that blank façade, holding his true reaction secret from me.

"Why would you not tell me I was ruining your career?"

He took a deep breath...and then released it, carefully. "You haven't ruined my career."

"But I've ruined all your prospects, haven't I?"

"Harwood..."

"*Your supervisor* told me so, Wrexham. In no uncertain terms." I tried to give a humorless laugh, but it caught painfully in my throat. "Trust me, I couldn't have mistaken his meaning."

At that, Wrexham winced and reached out as if to touch my face. "Don't let Westgate make you miserable over this. You know he has old-fashioned ideas. He—"

"But why didn't you *tell* me?" I demanded, jerking back. My voice was rising; I couldn't help it. "Didn't you think I would even care?"

Did *everyone* think me so self-absorbed? Even him?

"Of course I knew you would care," Wrexham snapped, dropping his hand. "For God's sake, Harwood, why do you *think* I didn't tell you? You already gave me up against my will once before, because you were so determined to protect me. Do you think I'd hand you *any* excuse to do that to me again? *Ever*?"

I stared down at him, stunned. "You're that certain I would have chosen my school over you?"

"I *know* you—wait. No." Wrexham closed his eyes, his chest rising and falling in a ragged breath beneath me. "This isn't the right way for us to discuss it. *Damn* it!"

Damn it, indeed.

Silently, I shifted aside until I was propped on one elbow on the mattress beside him. It was more than large enough for two people; it had been built as a marriage-bed, after all. We didn't even have to touch to share it.

Wrexham expelled a long, deep breath, keeping his eyes firmly closed. Dark shadows spread beneath his eyelashes, unmistakable marks of exhaustion. "Harwood," he said, "*my* Harwood. Do we truly have to discuss this right now? I can only stay for one night. I have to be gone again in the morning—"

"So we won't have another chance before you leave." I swallowed down a hard, swollen knot in my throat as my gaze traced the black stubble growing on his lean cheeks. No wonder he was exhausted; he'd been fighting off magical disasters for weeks, and he'd used even more energy to transport himself here tonight, only to do it again in just a few more hours.

No wonder Mr. Westgate was so angry on his behalf.

A better wife—a less selfish wife—would set aside hard truths for the sake of letting him rest. But the thought of sending him away for even more weeks of aching separation with this poisonous question simmering, toxic and unresolved between us...

"If I had told you," Wrexham said wearily, his eyes still closed, "you would have responded in one of only two possible ways. You could have given me up—*again*—and it would have broken me. I mean it, Harwood. I can't go through that again."

I let out a growl of vexation. "Wrexham—"

"*Or*," he continued implacably, "you could have given up your school for my sake...and that would have broken *you*." His eyes finally opened, unshielded and vulnerable, exposing himself to me utterly. "I know you, Harwood. I know what this chance means to you. It's your future."

"But what about what *you* mean to me, you fool?" I pushed one hand hard against his lean shoulder, biting back angry tears. "Don't you think I care about *your* dreams? *Your* future?"

The career he'd built for himself was nigh-on miraculous for a boy born into a poor sailor's family on the grimy seaside docks of Brigg Stow. His mother and his much older sisters had spent most of their lives working for a pittance in other people's ships, while his soft-spoken, poetical father had kept house with his son and earned eye-wateringly tiny wages through tutoring their neighbors in his native Marathan.

Wrexham had never attended any of the famous preparatory schools created for gentlemen's sons like my brother; instead, he'd fought his way into the Great Library through scholarships, determination, and inarguable skill. The fact that he'd then gone on to join the most elite and highly-paid force of magic-workers in the nation wasn't testimony to his talent alone; it was the result of decades of hard work and driving ambition.

He deserved every honor Mr. Westgate had ever predicted for him.

...And suddenly, I understood exactly why his mother and sisters hadn't replied to any of the dutiful letters I'd sent them since our wedding day. By now, they must resent me just as much as Westgate did.

"*Don't*," Wrexham told me now, with soft intensity. His dark eyes had narrowed, fixing on my face. "I know that look, Harwood. You're about to make some grand gesture, and I won't have it."

"I will *never* give you up again. Don't you dare even imagine it!" I glowered down at him, trying to beam the obvious truth into his maddeningly hard head. "Doing that once nearly shattered me. I don't have enough willpower to push you away a second time."

"For which we are *all* exceedingly thankful." His voice was dry, but his dark eyes gleamed, and his hands rose to cup my face with aching tenderness. "But, darling Harwood, I'm telling you now and I sincerely mean it: do *not* give up your school. Not for me. Not ever. That would poison our marriage irrevocably, and you know it."

"How is losing *your* career to my dreams any different?" A sob built up in my throat as I shifted closer, helplessly drawn into his gaze. We had always fit so perfectly together. We'd been *made* for each other; I knew it with all my heart.

So how could my dreams be fatal to his?

A sudden hammering at the door made me startle like a cat.

"Miss Harwood!" Miss Banks's voice was filled with panic. "You have to come and see this. *Now!*"

Miss Banks didn't blink an eyelid at my unbound hair, or at the sight of Wrexham behind me in the doorway. But then, my oldest and most seemingly sensible student had the unmistakable look of a woman torn from a romantic assignation of her own. Her fair blonde hair had been awkwardly re-pinned into a far simpler style than she'd worn earlier, and the three pearl buttons on her bodice—I couldn't help but notice—had been mis-buttoned since I had seen her last, revealing a shocking hint of white cotton underneath.

Apparently, the political Miss Fennell had been *far* more enthusiastic about their personal reunion than I could have guessed from her chilly public demeanor that day.

I automatically glanced down at myself to check for any such tell-tale mistakes in my own attire—but Miss Banks was already whirling around and starting toward the public staircase. "This way!"

Wrexham cocked one eyebrow at me in enquiry; I hesitated, then nodded firmly.

With the Boudiccate's inspectors lurking ominously nearby, and no notion of what was waiting for me, it would be madness to refuse his magical assistance. More importantly—marital issues notwithstanding—if I had only a few hours to spend with my husband, I wouldn't give up a single minute of his company.

Wrexham stayed a careful half a pace behind me as I followed Miss Banks down the corridor and broad public staircase. Still, the heat of his presence made the skin on my arms prickle, and I could feel his watchful gaze sweeping the space around us with professional intensity. It wasn't how I'd planned to introduce him to the renovations that I'd made to our new home—but it was an undeniable relief to have his silent support at my back.

Miss Banks led us at a swift pace through the maze of rooms on the ground floor to a room I hadn't yet shown any of my students. I'd planned to gather them all there tomorrow morning, after breakfast...but the library door stood open already, and the voice I heard through it made my jaw clench.

"My goodness, Caroline, I never imagined you'd develop any interest in magic yourself!" Annabel Renwick's light, edged laugh held every bit of lurking menace that I remembered from countless private encounters in my past—and Miss Banks paled at the sound, coming to a sudden halt with her hand already stretched out toward the door.

"She can't—she *mustn't* see us!" she whispered. "If she finds any proof of me and Caroline—!"

Annabel wasn't the *expected* crisis, then. She must have simply come snooping through the house with—as usual—the most horrific timing possible.

Never mind. I wasn't about to let her frighten any of my girls. Giving Miss Banks a firm nod, I swept toward the door —and whispered in her ear as I passed, *"Fix your buttons before you come in!"*

Miss Banks dropped her hands to her bodice with a gasp, and I stalked through the door with Wrexham at my heels.

Miss Fennell stood by the fireplace, which lay cold at this time of night, with no visitors expected. Her own gown was perfectly done up, her strong shoulders squared and her expression composed, and she held her hands loosely behind her back—a natural pose for reporting to her superior.

When I cast a quick glance about the room, I saw

nothing to alarm me—no faults exposed to Annabel's rapacious view—but when I looked back, I finally caught the hint of redness lurking on Miss Fennell's cheeks.

Her gaze fixed on me with unmistakable relief. "Miss Harwood."

"Miss Fennell." I nodded graciously. "And *dear* Annabel." It was the first time I'd ever addressed her by her first name, and I enjoyed the flaring of her nostrils in offense as I granted her a brief, dismissive nod. "Have you come looking for late-night reading? I could recommend a few introductory texts, if you're curious."

"Hardly." Annabel gave a disdainful sniff. "*Some* of us are successful enough in our own sphere that we needn't go rooting around gentlemen's leavings to make ourselves interesting. Isn't that right, Caroline?"

Miss Fennell blinked rapidly, her jaw flexing, and did not respond.

"But then..." Annabel's gaze rested pointedly on my unbound hair as her lips curved into a knowing smirk. "Perhaps I should be asking what *your* purpose is tonight, Miss Harwood. Is your own school library really the most appropriate place for evening assignations?" Her gaze moved smoothly past me to Wrexham. "I wonder—would Lionel Westgate be pleased to discover where his wayward protégé is tonight, when he's meant to be working halfway across the country?"

"Oh, come off it, Annabel." Rolling my eyes, I strode across the room to plant myself on a comfortable bronze-colored wingchair with the weight and presence of a throne. "You can hardly blackmail me over spending a private evening with my own husband. And Lionel Westgate is far too wise for your games. You may invite him to join us right now, if you'd like. Wrexham? *Are* you escaping any of your work by being here?"

"Not noticeably." Wrexham rested one hand lightly on my shoulder as he stepped into place beside my chair. "More's the pity," he added, and I had to restrain an unexpected snort of laughter.

"We *were* planning," I said, buoyed by that laughter, "to look through the texts here together and choose the best to pass on to an advanced student for her private study. If only we hadn't found the library so cluttered with politicians…" I sighed pointedly, then raised my voice, looking toward the open doorway. "It's all right, Miss Banks! You may safely enter now. I'm sure our friends from the Boudiccate won't stay too much longer…that is, if they really do find magic so tedious as they've always claimed."

Miss Banks hurried obediently into the room, her downturned face pink but her buttons perfectly lined up. There was nothing that could be done about her disordered hair, but as she took her place in the chair beside mine, even the most suspicious eye couldn't have drawn any connection between her and Miss Fennell, whose indifferent gaze passed over her without pause.

"The Boudiccate," said Annabel, "has no need for any *lessons*. But certainly…" She smiled pityingly at my student as she stepped away from the mantelpiece, dusting off her hands. "You must take advantage of these unheard-of opportunities whilst you have them. Within a handful of days—one never knows, does one?—they may be gone for good, and all memory of this hopeless little school along with them.

"Caroline?" She tilted her dark head at Miss Fennell. "Do walk me back to my room, if you please. I believe we have need of a private conversation."

"Certainly," said Miss Fennell woodenly, and gave my side of the room a curtsy. "Miss Harwood...Mr. Wrexham...Miss Banks."

At our polite murmurs of response, both politicians left the room.

The door closed behind their elegant figures.

"Phew." I slumped against the wide, padded back of my chair, and Wrexham gave my shoulder a comforting squeeze. "Thank goodness that's over!"

"But it's *not*," Miss Banks said. "She'll be going on at Caroline all the way back to their rooms. She's a nightmare! And she has Lady Cosgrave entirely under her thumb, which gives her free rein to make Caroline's life a misery."

"Oh, really?" My eyebrows shot upwards. "I never knew Lady Cosgrave to bend to anyone—and I never thought she cared for any of Annabel Renwick's opinions."

"She has to, now, whether she likes it or not. Didn't you notice how she treated your sister-in-law, who was her dearest friend for so long? Caroline thinks she must be acting on Mrs. Renwick's orders by cutting that particular connection." Miss Banks's face tightened. "I don't know what Mrs. Renwick is holding over Lady Cosgrave, but she's been sniffing after Caroline's own secrets for months now and harassing her at every chance she gets. If she works out our plans and tells the others before I've safely graduated with a degree in magic to make myself a suitable match..."

She shook her head, her face flushed with distress. "Lady Cosgrave would force Caroline to choose between me and her career in politics, I know it! She never minded Caroline preferring women—Caroline suspects she might secretly prefer them herself—but she's always said that a woman has to give up any dreams of romance to claim a place in the Boudiccate. So she gave up her own romances before she was married, and as far as she knows now, Caroline is planning to find herself a suitable magician husband soon as well. She *must* continue to believe that until we're in a strong enough position to stand against her and the others who feel the same way."

Wrexham's fingers worked at the knotted muscles in my shoulder even as he frowned at Miss Banks. "Surely, though, when it comes to her own niece—"

"She wouldn't even vote for Mrs. Harwood to join the Boudiccate, though they were such close friends at the time. She cast the deciding vote in that decision. And she even likes Mrs. Harwood's husband! But she says a marriage based on Boudicca's, matching politics to magic, is the price every member of the Boudiccate must pay for the sake of the nation as a whole. And now, just when I've finally found a way to gain magical credentials for myself..."

She gestured despairingly at the heavy green velvet curtains that covered the windows on the far side of the room. "Look at what we discovered!"

I twisted in my chair to follow her gaze, frowning. The lovely, braided silver sashes that I'd chosen so carefully hung limply at each side of the curtained windows, not hooked into place as my servants would have left them.

"Clever of Miss Fennell," Wrexham murmured. "She must have closed the curtains as soon as she heard Mrs. Renwick's approach."

"Actually..." Miss Banks gave a small cough. "Those curtains were closed when we arrived. It wasn't until we went to hide behind them ourselves that we discovered—well..." She gestured, sighing helplessly. "You'll have to see it for yourself."

Exchanging a wary look with my husband, I rose from my chair.

Together, we approached the windows. I could sense Wrexham readying his spells in preparation. A year ago, I would have been doing the same, just as I'd done a hundred times before...but I set my jaw and pushed that useless, too-familiar frustration aside.

"One...two...three!"

We jerked the curtains together, one on each side. They swooshed open between us in a rush...

And I sucked in a sharp breath as a makeshift altar was revealed upon the windowsill of my own school library.

An acorn, a foxglove, a heart-shaped leaf, a sparkling silver ring, and worst of all, three unmistakable drops of red human blood, none of them yet dry...oh, and there: a sprawling green spot smudged beside them.

The most dangerous sort of fey contract had been signed —and whatever the details of that agreement might be, it could only spell disaster for all of us.

6

The first several pulls of the housekeeping bell garnered no response, but the privacy of Miss Birch's room was inviolable. I forced myself to wait, pacing back and forth across the thick green carpet, until she finally appeared at the door wearing a faded dressing gown and a scowl.

"Well? My working hours are—ahh!" Her thin face tightened and her eyes flared, like a falcon who'd just caught sight of prey. Without another word or glance at any of us, she stalked to the windowsill where the illicit altar lay, untouched and waiting for her professional inspection.

Wrexham had been sitting in the bronze wingchair, poring through a thick book on fey lore, but he used one finger to mark his place and turned his watchful attention to my housekeeper as she glowered down at the offerings laid there.

She was a higher authority on the fey than any book stored in a library, for her combined heritage was an open secret in the neighborhood, one never discussed with outsiders. It was why she could command an eye-watering salary from anyone clever enough to value safety and comfort over the outmoded old prejudices that had ruled Anglish society for so long.

"In *my house*!" she snapped. "Of all the outrageous—!"

"So, you didn't feel it happen?" I asked.

It was a tactless question; I realized that too late as she swung toward me, her hazel eyes taking on an inhuman glitter. "D'you think I would have allowed a sneaking stranger in here on *purpose*, Miss Harwood?"

"No! No," I said hastily, "of course you wouldn't. I only wondered…" I cast desperately for an excuse. If only Amy were here!

My gaze landed on my husband, who rose to the occasion. "Now we know, then," Wrexham said calmly to Miss Birch, "that at least one of our bargainers must have used magic to hide this transaction from you."

"Not human magic," said Miss Birch. "I'd taste *that* in the air if they'd used it. But whoever they summoned with this nasty bit of work…" She gestured toward the altar, thin lips twisting as if she'd bitten into something sour. "*They* have power enough, oh, yes, they do."

"Can you taste their magic?" I stepped closer, tensing. "Enough to identify what they are?"

"Ha." She hunched a dismissive shoulder. "You think a creature that powerful can't hide their true nature? All *I* taste in here…" She sniffed the air, then rolled her eyes at my oldest student. "Apart from the obvious fol-de-rol, that is…"

Miss Banks flushed and lifted one hand to her buttons, as if checking they were once again safely closed.

"There's only one other taste still lingering," said Miss Birch. "*Malice*. Whoever was summoned, they came for the joy of wreaking havoc, and that's exactly what they were summoned to do. *Someone* isn't a friend of this school of yours, Miss Harwood."

"'Someone?'" Groaning, I threw myself down onto a stool by the fireplace and dug my fingers hard through my unbound hair. "Try *everyone*, Miss Birch. Apart from my students and staff..."

"Can you even be sure of them?" Wrexham asked quietly. "If one of your students or your servants was planted here as a spy—or believes they're doing some good for the nation by sabotaging this venture before it can upset the status quo..."

I was shaking my head before he finished speaking. "If you'd spoken to those girls, you would *know* their sincerity! They've all fought to teach themselves magic over the years, working in secret and in spite of every prohibition. They are ecstatic at the thought of finally learning more! I know what that joy sounds like, Wrexham. I believe them."

"And *my* staff," said Miss Birch, "haven't left their own quarters since lights-out over an hour ago. You can be quite sure of that, I assure you, sir!"

"Those drops of blood can't be more than an hour old," said Wrexham, "so I'll accept that they couldn't have been left by any staff members, if they've all been in their quarters this whole time. But Harwood..."

He sighed as he looked across at me. "I know you see yourself in these girls. But don't forget: every girl in Angland for centuries has been raised to aspire to the Boudiccate, not to the Great Library—no matter what her own natural abilities might be. So, if anyone in the Boudiccate wished to insert a trusted spy within your ranks—"

"I don't believe it." Miss Banks sat stiffly upright, her fair brows knotted and all signs of her earlier embarrassment gone. "We all gathered together in our common room tonight after Miss Harwood's talk. There was no one amongst us who wasn't desperate to be here—*and* for this school to succeed. I could swear to it!"

"When you met Miss Fennell for your rendezvous," said Wrexham, "did you come here directly from that meeting?"

She nodded. "I told the others that I wanted a walk on my own before bed."

"Then the two of you must have arrived just after the summoning had finished, because that blood was still wet when you brought us here. Were you the first to leave that gathering of students tonight?"

"I think...oh." Her shoulders slumped. "No," she said. "Two other girls left before me—Miss Stewart and Miss Hammersley. But I'm certain neither of them would have done this. They're too happy to be here—and too eager for our proper classes to start. Miss Hammersley hasn't even managed to hunt down any decent spellbooks back home, and Miss Stewart is frantic to start her real work at weather-wizardry. She couldn't stop talking about how fortunate we are to have Mr. Luton here!"

"Mm," I said, and hoped that my neutral syllable covered Miss Birch's derisive sniff. "So, seven of my nine students have alibis already. I'm sure we'll rule out the other two soon enough."

"It would be interesting," Wrexham said, closing the book in his lap and setting it aside on a low table, "to find out exactly how much research either of those two students had done on fey lore before they came here. You might try to find that out when you question them tomorrow, Harwood."

Question them? I rolled my shoulders irritably. "They're hardly criminals," I said. "They're my *students*. Of course I'll talk with them, but you know as well as I that neither of them is the most likely suspect. For that, we are looking at the people who came here *specifically* with the purpose of shutting down my school. What could possibly serve them better than to summon a fey to cause mischief now, in the midst of our inspection?"

"It wasn't Caroline!" Miss Banks shot upright, her cheeks flushing. "*Please* don't even think to suggest such a thing! She was every bit as shocked as I was to find that awful altar. And actually"—she brightened, giving me a triumphant look—"*she* was the one who said I should run and get you as quickly as possible, even though it meant giving up all of our private time together. *And* she needs this school to succeed for her sake, too!"

Oh, young love. With an effort, I withheld a weary eye-roll. "I was not," I said, "referring to your fiancée, Miss Banks. I was thinking, instead, of the woman who is doing her best to blackmail your fiancée as we speak. Annabel Renwick has no conscience whatsoever, and she's every bit as malicious as any fey, so—*oh.*" I cringed, turning back to my housekeeper. "I do beg your pardon—"

"*That* kind of creature," said Miss Birch, pointing at the windowsill, "*is* malicious, and there's no doubting it. But if you have any opinions you'd care to share now on peaceful, law-abiding fey, who hold to the old agreements and want nothing more than—"

"I don't!" I said fervently. "I truly do not. My tongue ran away with me, but that is no excuse. I was unforgivably rude, and I sincerely apologize. I'll owe you even more apologies later, when we have time, if you'd like—"

"No, thank you," said my housekeeper drily. "The one's enough, if you mean it—*and* if you don't say it again."

"I won't. I promise you." I swallowed down bitter regret.

What I'd said so thoughtlessly a moment ago was just the sort of line I'd heard tossed around in neighborhood social gatherings a hundred times as I'd grown up, surrounded by humans, with the fey known only through warning stories from our woods. Their official ambassadress had been an annual, exotic visitor at Mother's Spring Equinox ball, but she'd been far too distant, glittering and intimidating to quash any local fears.

Still, I knew better, by now, than to repeat any such prejudicial nonsense myself. It had been nearly thirty years since the first fey-human marriage had been legally recognized. For all that matches like the one between Miss Birch's parents were still viewed by closed-minded people as shocking, they were hardly unheard-of anymore. Besides, there were more different types of fey than any other creature in the nation. It was horrendously unfair to tar them all with the same brush, and I never would have done so if I had been thinking at full capacity.

Exhaustion was catching up with me after nine nearly sleepless nights, making me start to slip in far too many ways—and it was exactly what I could least afford with so many unfriendly eyes judging my new school.

I tipped my head forward, letting my own eyes fall closed as I rubbed at my forehead with my fingertips, trying to massage away the growing ache of tiredness and gnawing anxiety.

I still had to come up with a new lesson plan for tomorrow, somehow, amidst all this chaos...if, that was, we actually managed to *have* a lesson, and that mysterious fey bargain didn't scuttle everything beforehand.

"If any politician was discovered to have entered into a blood-bargain with a fey against a fellow human," said Wrexham, "she wouldn't only lose her career, she might well face a prison sentence, no matter how high her standing might be. Do you think Mrs. Renwick truly cares so much about your school, to risk such a dire fate for herself?"

"It would certainly explain why she was poking around in here," I muttered. My eyes were still closed, and a faint buzz sounded, high and distracting, in my ears as the room began to gently sway around me. "If she left in a hurry when she heard Miss Banks and Miss Fennell coming, then tried to come back to collect the evidence... Did anyone happen to recognize that silver ring on the altar?"

"I didn't *see* anyone wearing it today," said Miss Banks doubtfully, "although it is so plain, perhaps I could have overlooked it."

"It means something important to *someone*," I said, without opening my eyes. "Otherwise, it could never have been used to seal a blood-bargain." Such bargains might have been forbidden for centuries, but the whispered stories of their dangers—and their rules—had been passed through every new generation in this southern part of Angland. A lesser bargain might have been agreed upon for a mere trinket, but a blood-bargain demanded a true sacrifice...and not in monetary terms.

If it meant so much to our attacker on an emotional level, though, why hadn't she been wearing it earlier today? I might not trust my own observational skills when it came to fashion, but as neither Miss Banks nor Miss Birch had noticed it either, I could be fairly certain it hadn't been visible on any lady's finger.

In the morning, I would have to ask Amy if she had glimpsed the ring herself—but the mere thought of waking her now to ask that question made me cringe. Self-absorbed though I might be, even I knew better than to rouse a nursing mother who almost never managed real sleep anymore.

As Mr. Westgate had pointed out, I'd dragged Amy into more than enough of my troubles already.

"Now the bargain's been sealed, that ring belongs to its new owner," said Miss Birch grimly. "It can't be collected until the deed is done, but *that*'s all it reeks of now on first sniff—blood and fixed intention. Nasty stuff."

Wrexham said something more, but his words blurred together with Miss Banks's response. My elbows dug into my legs, two distant points of discomfort, as I tipped forward on the stool.

Acorns and leaves and bloody thorns, tangling around me...

Wrexham's voice broke into my consciousness. "...I won't be leaving tonight, after all."

"What?" I jerked upwards, blinking myself awake. My husband knelt just beside me on the carpet, his long arms stretched out as if to catch me if I fell. "What did you just say?" I demanded.

"Did you really not hear?" He smiled quizzically, his expression tender. "I won't be leaving you tonight."

"Why—? *Oh*." Of course.

Wrexham was an officer of magic for the Boudiccate. He'd never willingly walk away from such a puzzle. Unfortunately, he might not have the choice.

I shook my head muzzily, trying to pull my fragmented thoughts together. "They'll call in someone else as soon as we tell them about it. They'd never let you be the one to manage it."

"*Can* we even tell them?" Miss Banks asked worriedly. "If they're looking for any excuse to shut down Thornfell..."

A shiver rippled through me at the thought. If the

Boudiccate's inspectors claimed that the school was now unsafe...

"We don't even know what that cursed bargain *was*!" I groaned. "If we find out, after all this, that they were only bargaining for a fey to tie our hair to our beds at night, or some such..."

"There was blood on that altar," said Wrexham grimly. "That was no mere agreement to tease or to trick."

"Well, they're not getting away with even that much in *my* house!" Miss Birch's small figure seemed to grow, like a tree stretching out sharp branches, as she planted herself before us, elbows sticking out from her crossed arms and her shadow expanding farther and farther along the carpet behind her. "They may have snuck past me tonight, but I'm on the lookout for them now. They won't be breaking *my* boundaries again without notice!"

Wrexham looked her steadily in the eye from his kneeling position. "I have full faith in that assurance, Miss Birch, but the true question is: can you actually stop them once you feel them coming?"

The wrinkles in her face turned deeper, but she didn't answer...which was an answer in itself.

I sighed and pushed myself up off my stool, shoving down all my exhaustion. *Time to take charge.* "Miss Birch's alert should give us enough time to go to Mr. Westgate, at least—and *he* can summon help even if he's still too drained to manage any magic himself."

"He won't need to summon anyone," said Wrexham, "if I'm here."

"But that," I said flatly, "cannot happen."

After weeks of separation, I wanted to snatch at any excuse, no matter how slight, to keep him by my side. But Lionel Westgate's earlier words echoed in my ears now as I looked down at Wrexham, who still knelt by my side where he'd offered his support—support that anyone in Angland would be mad to refuse.

But I was mad about *him*—so I couldn't possibly accept. "I'll follow your earlier instructions," I told him, "and not give up my school for you—but you will *not* give up your career for me, either. I won't have it!"

Wrexham's jaw set in aggravatingly stubborn lines as he rose to loom over me. "It's hardly *giving up my career* to investigate a magical mystery as an officer of the Boudiccate—"

"—Who has been ordered to deal with other magic, else-where," I snapped. "The Boudiccate are *looking* for an excuse to be rid of you, Wrexham. They can't sack you outright for no reason—so for heaven's sake, don't give them one! If you actually refuse to follow their orders, even Mr. Westgate won't be able to protect you."

"The devil take Westgate *and* my career!" Wrexham snarled. "If you think I'm going to leave you at the mercy of whatever that summoned creature may be, with no active magician in the house to defend you—"

"I beg your pardon?" I narrowed my eyes up at him, crossing my arms between us. "Do you *really* think me entirely helpless, only because I can no longer cast any magic of my own?"

"Um." Miss Banks coughed frantically beside us. "Miss Harwood...Mr. Wrexham...that is, there *are* other magicians in this school. Nine of us! We may not be trained yet, but we are practicing. Couldn't magical defenses be some of our first lessons here?"

"No!" Wrexham and I both chorused the denial in unison. My husband looked ready to explain, but I got in first. "Magical defenses don't begin until the *second* year of study," I said firmly, "but more importantly: you will *never* be required to defend yourself from danger at my school. You are my students, and *I* will keep you all safe while you're here."

"But—"

"Oh, don't worry yourself," said Miss Birch briskly. "I might not be able to defeat that creature, but I can certainly keep it busy enough while a trained magician is summoned to deal with it. We won't be needing to drag any young ladies into this...*or* you, either, sir," she added kindly, with a nod to Wrexham. "You needn't worry for your wife's safety in *this* house."

"Or *ever*," I added under my breath.

Wrexham gave me a look of utter exasperation.

In the corner, the clock tolled a long, mournful sound. Automatically, I glanced at the time...and winced.

"Miss Birch," I said, "may I leave the safe disposal of that...*thing*...to your care?" I waved at the altar on the window, not bothering to hide my disgust.

"Oh, trust me," she said grimly. "It will be a *pleasure*. I'll keep that ring safe, too, and locked up tight."

"Wonderful. And do please see if you can ferret out any leftover kinships still linking it to anyone in this household." A mere human spell could never reveal such subtle details, but fey magic was a powerful and sidelong force. It was the best I could hope for, at the moment. "Miss Banks"—I turned to my student—"I'll see you in class tomorrow. And you need your sleep, so no more secret meetings beforehand, if you please! Wrexham..." I gestured toward the door.

"As you say," said my husband, and walked silently by my side all the way back up to our bedroom.

To an outside observer, he might have looked calm and absorbed in distant thoughts, but I had known him for years, and I could feel his frustration like a dark, close fog in the air around us, no matter how hard he tried to disguise it. So I sighed as I closed the door behind us, and I braced myself for continued battle.

"I know you'd rather stay and deal with all of this your-self," I said, "but you know as well as I do, if you want to keep your position—"

"One day, Harwood," said Wrexham sharply, "you might consider *not* deciding what's best for me no matter what I say about the matter." As I gaped at him, stunned into momentary silence, he added with an unconvincing attempt at lightness, "I *am* surprisingly capable of making those decisions for myself—as I have tried to explain to you, once or twice before across the last several years."

Hurt battled with anger in my chest, making it difficult to speak. Finally, I managed, "*Everyone* knows that you're brilliant—there's no question that you're qualified to make your own decisions. But if you sacrifice your own goals for mine—"

"Then that will be *my* decision," he said through his teeth, "and I won't blame you for it."

"Oh, no?" I demanded. "So you've changed your mind, and you won't reproach me if I sacrifice *my* dreams and my school for you, now? Since you wouldn't dream of telling *me* what's best for myself, either?"

There was a long, pulsating moment of silence.

Then Wrexham tipped his head forward with a sigh. "Oh, Harwood." Shoulders relaxing, he gave me a rueful smile. "We truly are a pair, aren't we?"

"Always." I stepped forward and closed my arms tightly around his lean body, relief coursing through my veins. "I'm not trying to order you around," I mumbled into his chest. "I just want to look after you, because you're so stubborn, you'll never do it for yourself."

"...Said the pot to the kettle. Darling hypocrite." He let out a puff of laughter in my ear. "In other words, we are a perfect match...and we'll keep squabbling over each other's welfare for another fifty years or more if we're fortunate."

"But not if you drive yourself into the ground first!" Pushing him back a reluctant inch, I used one forefinger to trace the deep lines under his eyes. "You need to sleep," I said sadly, "and regain your energy before you start your work for the day. You know I want you desperately, but—"

"I'm staying," he said, "until dawn." I frowned, preparing to argue, but he shook his head at me. "It's a compromise," he said softly. "We will sleep, I promise. We'll *only* sleep, because we *both* need the rest—I saw you falling asleep on that stool earlier!—and then I'll leave the very moment that dawn arrives. I'll protect myself for your sake, as you'll protect yourself for mine. No one will fault my attendance *or* my work. But, my Harwood..."

His fingertips brushed against my face with unbearable tenderness, his dark gaze holding mine and pulling me closer into his thrall. "What I want," he murmured, "more than anything else in the world, is to fall asleep with my arms around my wife. I just want us to give ourselves this single night of resting *together*. Do you think we could agree on that?"

"Ohhh." I pressed my face into his chest to keep my unruly expression under control. "You have *no idea* how happy I am to agree to that!"

And I fell asleep only fifteen minutes later, despite all the hot, tingling temptation of his proximity. I wrapped myself in the comfort and strength of his deliciously bare arms and sank into pure blackness, smiling...

Until the dream, as always, began.

There was never any adequate way to prepare for it—and tonight, I was caught horribly off-guard, eased into complacency by Wrexham's presence. So the nightmare sucked me into its maw before I could even try to escape...

And this time, I wasn't alone in it.

7

"Aaah!" I launched myself upright, one hand clawing at my own throat as I reached frantically with my other hand for Wrexham.

My fingers landed on a cold, bare sheet instead of skin.

Wrexham's side of the bed was empty. I stared at the rumpled space where he should have been, my heartbeat rattling, as dream and reality mingled terrifyingly together.

Thorns wrapping around him, piercing his skin as I screamed and fought to tear myself free from my own bindings. His dark eyes flaring wide with shock and pain, and then—

No!

It was a dream and no more, just as always. No cruel thorns pierced my own throat now that I was awake; no bloody marks showed along my skin where piercing vines had seemed to pin me moments earlier.

Sunlight filtered in through the curtains, lighting the room. Wrexham had simply left, as promised, at dawn, leaving me to sleep on...and that cursed dream had kept me buried too deep in its smothering embrace to even hear my husband leave. That was all.

It was all that it could be.

I let out a muffled scream of frustration. If *only* I could cast a simple spell to check his safety! I would have given anything for that reassurance right now. Dread crawled through me with every breath, like spiders creeping across my skin, whispering threats and warnings...

...Which was patently absurd. It was only a dream!

Taking a deep breath, I scooped a hairbrush from my side table and yanked it hard through my thick hair as I pulled the cord to summon my maid. Just by where the hairbrush had lain, I spotted a scrap of paper startlingly out of place; with a gush of relief, I recognized the sloping handwriting across it.

Take care of yourself for my sake, will you, darling Harwood? I'm still waiting for our wedding night. - W

There! I brushed my fingers against it, letting out my breath. No vines had stolen him from our bed; he'd merely left me to sleep, considerate as always. So he was absolutely *fine*, no matter what that devilish dream had made me fear. It was time to leave behind the murky land of dreams and see what nightmares awaited my school in waking life.

...Beginning with my first class in front of the Boudiccate's inspectors.

I'd planned to begin with a stirring five-minute lecture that would have lit a fire in any young woman magician— but it would have outraged any member of the Boudiccate. So, with my critical new audience members in mind, I regretfully crossed out that plan over a hasty private breakfast.

As I'd told Wrexham only a few hours ago, there was no point in handing the Boudiccate any gift-wrapped excuses to be rid of us. But it was with a sense of vengeful satisfaction that I decided to begin my first class, instead, with a simple demonstration of every politically inconvenient truth that I had planned to blast out in that original speech.

"Miss Hammersley," I said as my students took their whispering, giggling places in Thornfell's back parlor. The air jangled with their gathered excitement and nerves, a chaotic, nearly tangible force that sent goosebumps skittering across my skin. "Would you please join me at the front of the room?"

Miss Hammersley gulped, while the other eight students rustled with interest. The Boudiccate's inspection team sat in the back corner, and Annabel Renwick raised one expressive eyebrow as she pointedly looked my most impoverished student up and down, from her plainly dressed red hair to the hem of her faded and much-mended dark blue gown.

As Miss Banks had told Wrexham, Miss Hammersley—one of my two students without an alibi for last night's mischief—hadn't had the opportunity to raid any libraries of magic in her own home. She'd grown up in a practical farming family with hardly any access to spells, so she had none of the cultural or magical experience so prized amongst the fashionable young gentlemen who arrived at the Great Library after years of preparation.

...Which served my purposes today exactly.

"Miss Harwood." Her pale green eyes were wide with what looked like panic, but her low voice was firm and beautifully resonant. She raised her strong, freckled chin high as she stood before me and clasped her hands together under the gazes of her classmates and our inspectors.

Brave girl. I gave her a small, approving nod.

It had taken courage to apply to my school by letter, too, as the first magician in her family, with no one to vouch for her suitability. Of course she couldn't pay the fee that Amy and I had settled on as both appropriate and impressive to families used to the Great Library's charges—but the passion and fierce intelligence in her letter had won her a place before I'd even finished reading it.

I was married to a former scholarship student. I knew exactly how little that web of aristocratic social connections really mattered when it came to a magician's true abilities— and *exactly* what it felt like to thirst for magic without an outlet.

"I'd like to perform an experiment," I said. "Miss Hammersley, would you please take up one of the textbooks from this table?" I gestured at the polished oak side table behind me, which was stacked with books of varying sizes.

She hesitated with one freckled and calloused hand hovering above the pile. "Does it matter which one I choose?"

"Not this time."

She bit her lip, then nodded decisively and scooped up a slim volume from the middle of the table.

"An excellent choice." I took it from her and held it up for the rest of the class to see. "This is Aguirre's *Elements of Spellcraft*—a book traditionally studied in the third year at the Great Library." Smiling, I passed it back to Miss Hammersley. "Why don't you open it to page fifty?"

Her throat moved with her swallow, but she did as I'd asked.

"Now," I said, "I'd like you to read it out loud."

For the first time, she balked. "Miss Harwood..." She took a deep breath, lowering her voice to a pained whisper. "I don't know any of these words."

"You don't need to...yet." I put one hand on her shoulder, ignoring our audience to firmly hold her gaze. "Trust me. I don't care about pronunciation or meaning. All I want you to focus on as you speak is your *will*."

"My...will?" She frowned as the other students leaned in, listening intently.

"Your will," I repeated firmly. "You have a strong will, Miss Hammersley. You *all* do, every one of you." I looked across my class, taking the time to meet each gaze in turn: nine young women of different heights, skin colors, fashions, and ages, all united in one room and one radical endeavor. "You wouldn't be brave enough to be here in Angland's first class of women magicians if you didn't."

I turned back to Miss Hammersley. "So don't allow yourself to worry about anything else. Right now, I want you to hold just one thing in your head: how desperately you want to be a magician...

"...Because you do, don't you?"

"More than anything in the world." Her voice was ragged with emotion. A sigh of empathy rippled through her classmates as she spoke, all of them leaning even closer.

"Then hold that in your head. Don't even think about the words or what they might mean. Just think about what *this* means to you, now: standing here, beginning your training amongst your peers." I gestured to the eight young women around us. "By the end of your four years here, I can promise you that the nine of you will have formed a bond that will be nigh-on unbreakable. And when women work together..." I let my gaze drift to the watching Boudiccate inspectors. My smile turned rueful as I nodded discreetly to them. "We *all* know what national wonders they can work."

Lady Cosgrave's eyes narrowed. Annabel Renwick looked sour, while Miss Fennell looked pleased. Mr. Westgate looked stoically unmoved as usual...

And Miss Hammersley's voice rolled through the room, firmly and clearly reading every word of the spell—with the full force of her impressive willpower behind it.

That was exactly what she needed.

Glorious, celebratory bells suddenly rang through the air, sending students and inspectors jumping in their seats. The invisible bells chimed rich and resonant around us, so loud and overwhelming that they almost drowned out the cries of surprise and laughter and delight that sounded throughout the whole class in response...

And tears of pride sprang to my eyes, mirroring the sparkling drops that rolled down Miss Hammersley's freckled cheeks as her own glorious and strong magic sang out in those bells, filling the room with music and power.

She read the entire spell from beginning to end without faltering even once.

"And *that*," I said, as the final echoes faded into a wonderstruck hush, "is what I want every one of you to remember over your next four years here. We will work on the intricacies of control. You will struggle to master every complexity that our vocation has to offer. You will memorize more finicky details than you can yet imagine...but at its essence? *This* is what magic requires, more than anything else: pure willpower and determination.

"And I *know* that every single one of you is capable of it.

"Now..." I plucked a well-worn book from a different table as Miss Hammersley strode back to her seat, her eyes shining and pride emanating from her like a visible sheen. "Let's go back and start from the very beginning to see exactly how a competent spell is crafted."

The basics could never be as exciting as a spell from a third-year textbook. But the glow of Miss Hammersley's triumph illuminated every student in her class. At the end of the hour, when they flooded out of the room for their first outdoor lesson in weather wizardry, their enthusiastic voices rose in an honor guard around her, carrying her at their center through the door.

I would *never* allow any scholarship students to be treated with less than full respect and collegiality at my school…and while Miss Hammersley might not yet have an alibi for the night before, my experiment had revealed one essential trust. No one who was only pretending to desire magic could have successfully cast that spell in that context, following those specific instructions.

If she was a spy for the Boudiccate, I would eat every one of my spellbooks—even the unforgivably ill-informed ones. But I didn't believe it would ever come to that.

I was smiling as I looked back from the now-empty doorway. The Boudiccate's inspectors, however, were not.

"Well!" said Annabel Renwick, shaking out the flowing skirts of her fey-silk gown as she rose to her feet. "You're still willing to risk anything and anyone to prove a point, aren't you? I should have thought you'd be a bit more careful when it comes to your students' welfare rather than your own."

"I beg your pardon?" A disbelieving crack of laughter fell out of my mouth before I could stop it. "How do you imagine I've put any of them in danger?"

Her upper lip curled as she studied me. "I seem to recall a certain arrogant woman magician losing all of her own magic—and nearly her life as well—when *she* attempted a spell far beyond her own abilities. To set a third-year exercise as a first spell for one of your own students now…"

I didn't even attempt to restrain my eye-roll at that nonsense. "You may ask Mr. Westgate, if you like, how much *danger* I put Miss Hammersley in with that spell."

"None whatsoever," Mr. Westgate said curtly. "If she hadn't harnessed the willpower for that one, it simply wouldn't have had any effect. It's an entirely harmless exercise...as any graduate of the Great Library would know." He pointedly refused to meet my gaze as he rapped out his next question: "Where exactly is this next class being held?"

"In the courtyard just by Mr. Luton's cottage," I told him.

"Fine." He jerked a dismissive nod, still not meeting my gaze, and strode out of the room for the next inspection.

"Ah, young Luton. Poor, poor Delilah's nephew." Annabel sighed and shook her head as she swept past me. "I suppose I shouldn't be surprised by now at your...unusual taste in staff members."

"I suppose not," I agreed with outward amiability.

Unease slithered beneath my skin, though, as I watched her leave. If she was only disparaging me with that barb, I could endure it well enough; but if she'd somehow ferreted out any dangerous hints of my housekeeper's fey background and thought to make some mischief with it...

"Miss Harwood," said Lady Cosgrave, "a word, if you please."

"Of course." I snapped my attention back to the space in front of me, where Lady Cosgrave waited with her young cousin and protégée, Miss Fennell, standing rigid and expressionless by her side.

I'd only met Miss Fennell a few months ago through her secret fiancée, but Lady Cosgrave had been one of the prominent figures of my youth. Fashionable, charming, and quick-thinking, she had been twenty years younger than my own mother, but the two of them had been on sociable terms even before she and Amy had formed a close friendship of their own. She and I had never had a personal relationship, but I'd always felt at ease in her company...until now.

I remembered the chill disdain on her face as she'd

dismissed my loyal, loving sister-in-law the day before, and my own expression set in rigid lines despite my best attempts to keep it neutral. "You wished to discuss my lesson plan, too?" I inquired.

She gave an irritated sniff. "Oh, really, Cassandra. Let's not waste our time in pointless fencing when we have only a few minutes to ourselves."

...Before she had to join Annabel Renwick, I assumed—and I remembered Miss Banks's words from last night. *"She has Lady Cosgrave entirely under her thumb."*

I would have felt more empathy for any woman under threat of blackmail if she hadn't saved herself by damning Amy and threatening my school.

"You may tell me whatever you came to say, Honoria." I turned away from her, gathering up my assorted books and tossing my words over my shoulder. "But let's not pretend to any privacy between ourselves, if you please. Anything I say to you will only be repeated to Annabel Renwick the moment she asks, won't it? She seems to have taken priority over all of your old friendships."

"Are *you* speaking to me of loyalty?" She let out a surprisingly bitter laugh. "I'm coming to you now to offer you this chance only because of my fondness for your family. You're still Miranda Harwood's daughter, whether you admit to it or not—so somewhere inside, no matter how deeply you've buried it, I *know* you must still have that sense of duty and of principle that your mother fought so hard to instill in you."

I was grateful that she couldn't see my expression with my back still safely turned. "This has indeed been a delightful conversation. However, if you'll excuse me, I have my next lesson to plan, and you—"

"You have *no idea* how much danger we're all in, if this

disastrous venture actually succeeds. Were you even watching those girls in your class this morning, eating up everything you fed them without a second thought?" Lady Cosgrave had always been famous for her charm, but her voice lashed out now like a whip. "This isn't some jolly girls' adventure club you're leading! It is a revolution that could topple *everything* England stands for."

"Oh, for—!" I bit off an intemperate curse as I swung around, clasping my gathered books to my chest. "Honoria, no one is trying to topple anything. Didn't you see the pure joy in those girls' faces?"

"I saw exactly what you'd planned to show us all in that little demonstration," she snapped. "I saw a tide of change that won't be turned unless you call a halt to it *now*, before it's too late. And I don't just mean closing this school; I mean going to the newspapers and telling every one of them that it was a terrible mistake ever to have conceived of it!"

At that, I laughed out loud, and my shoulders relaxed. "That is *never* going to happen," I assured her. "If you remember my mother at all, you should know better than to expect any daughter of hers to be cowardly."

"And what kind of future do you want for your own daughters?" Lady Cosgrave demanded. "Once we've lost every gain we made in the past *seventeen hundred and fifty* years?"

"I beg your pardon?" I blinked, looking past her to Miss Fennell. The younger woman's lips were pursed together, and I couldn't begin to guess at her true thoughts behind her lowered gaze. At last winter's house party, surrounded by friends her own age, she'd been loud and expansive, with all the flair and magnetism of a future leader, but in her subordinate role here as an assistant—with secrets in danger from more than one of her superiors—she was keeping herself unnaturally mute, all her vibrancy disheart-eningly repressed.

It felt wrong...and it was a reminder: I wasn't only fighting for my own students now.

"Look at the new Daniscan Republic," Lady Cosgrave told me. "Or the elven kingdom up north, cheek-by-jowl to Angland itself. *Or* half the nations on the continent, for that matter! What do they all have in common?" She answered her own question before I could: "*Men*. They rule *everything*. Do you have any idea how easily that could happen here as well?"

"Don't be absurd. From Boudicca onwards, we have *always*—"

"Because we had an agreement!" she snarled. "An agreement that *both sides* followed without exception. I *told* your mother even one woman magician was too many—but those girls in your class are a tipping point that will crash our ship entirely."

Behind her, Miss Fennell's lips opened as if to speak—but Lady Cosgrave swept straight past whatever diplomatic protest her younger cousin might have offered.

"How many months do you think it will take," she demanded, "for the first opinion pieces to arrive in the national newspapers, insisting that gentlemen be allowed to enter politics now that our old agreement has been broken? And how much longer do you think it'll be before people start to say the gentlemen would do a *better job* of it on their own?"

"They couldn't," I said flatly. "Everyone who's studied history can *see* what a remarkable job we've done."

"Ha! The general public," said Lady Cosgrave, "doesn't care a jot for history. All they want is to feel comfortable *now* —and just wait until the next unpopular decision about taxes or tariffs has to be made. Or the next economic recession! Some enterprising group of gentlemen is going to leap at that opportunity and start trumpeting their greater talents in the newspapers, *exactly* as you did when it came to your own self-aggrandizing demands."

I set my jaw and strove for patience. "I never said that women were naturally *better* magicians than men. I only said that we should be allowed—"

"*Half the world* is already ruled by men who claim we have no right to any power at all! Have you paid even the slightest attention to the way that women are treated in the elven kingdom? They aren't even allowed to choose their own husbands, let alone make decisions for their nation as a whole. I was the ambassadress there for three years, remember! I *saw* what they endure."

"And I believe you," I said sincerely.

Unlike the fey, the disdainful elves had never deigned to mingle with human society. Although our two nations were finally in the midst of an uneasy peace, the truth was that after all our long centuries of war, any true friendships would have been unthinkable even if any elves had been available to form them...and even then, no Anglish woman with any pride could have stomached them.

Elven gentlemen were only rarely glimpsed outside the secrecy of their own northern kingdom, and no elven ladies were ever allowed outside it. Still, I had heard horror stories all my life of the depth of their subjection. The punishments that those ladies received for any infractions of their oppressive laws were notorious throughout Angland for their brutality.

"But none of those other nations have been *ruled* by women for over seventeen hundred years. Moreover..." I frowned, thinking it through as levelly as I could. "If men *do* demand a place in politics to mirror women's acceptance in the field of magic...would that be such a terrible thing?"

It would be a shocking change, admittedly; an unsettling adjustment that would take some time even for me to wrap my own mind around. Like everyone else in Angland, I'd grown up with the firm and undisputed understanding that men were far too emotional and irrational to ever be trusted with practical governance.

But hadn't we also all been told that women were too rational and hard-headed to ever successfully work any magic?

"It's a new era for all of us," I said. "It may take some time for everyone to settle into our new positions. I imagine there will be controversies along the way. But Boudicca herself overthrew the government of this nation, sent the all-powerful Roman Empire packing, and devised a whole new form of governance despite what had *always been done* —so I don't think any of us nowadays have to be too cowardly to aim for *true* justice and equality, no matter which field we're speaking of.

"After all, if we refuse to even try...then how can we claim to be better than any of those other nations you just mentioned?"

Miss Fennell's eyes shone, but she pressed her lips together and lowered her head, waiting deferentially for her older cousin's response. Lady Cosgrave looked at me for a long, silent moment.

When she spoke again, her voice was bitter.

"I should have known," she said, "that you wouldn't care for anything but your personal ambitions, no matter how many other women's futures are shattered by your actions. You broke your own mother's heart when you refused her legacy all those years ago. Now you're ready to destroy it for every other woman in this nation, after all the work your mother and grandmother did to maintain our traditions and keep all of us safe.

"I'm disappointed in you, Cassandra...but I can't say I'm surprised." She swept towards the door, shaking her head. "Just remember: I offered you a chance to redeem yourself. I doubt that such a gift will be granted to you again."

With an apologetic look, Miss Fennell turned and followed after her older cousin.

As they walked together through the doorway, I stood alone with my books in my arms and those final words echoing around me.

8

A my found me ten minutes later as I sat in my office gazing sightlessly at a thick pile of papers on my desk. A quill pen in my hands dripped dark green ink that I hadn't yet begun to use.

"Cassandra? I—oh!" She gave a quizzical frown as I jerked, ink spraying across my pages, at the sound of her voice.

"I beg your pardon." Grimacing, I set down my pen and scooped up a cloth to dab at the spreading green spill. "I was in a haze."

"I can see that." Smiling ruefully, she stepped into the room, patting baby Miranda's back comfortingly. My little niece was securely propped against her mother's left shoulder, but she strained to turn her head toward me, tiny, light brown hands fluttering against Amy's striped morning gown. The glimpse I caught of her dark eyes looked mischievously alert.

"Isn't this her naptime?"

"So you might think." Amy rolled her eyes as she held out the wriggling, gurgling evidence. "But *this* little girl has decided she has no need of naps today after all, with so much excitement going on. So I thought I'd let her visit her aunt for a minute or two, as an excuse to catch up on all the gossip between classes."

"Oh, I know alllll about troublesome girls who just won't follow the rules!" I scooped Miranda from her mother's arms and snuggled her soft warmth into my chest as she cooed with delight, her bright gaze fixed on my face. The sight made my vision blur—so I hastily buried my face against her warm, soft brown curls to hide my expression from my sister-in-law. "We're the best kind, aren't we, little one?" I whispered to my niece.

Amy had always been far too astute at reading other people's feelings. It was what had made her such an excellent politician...at least until I had scuppered her career.

At the sound of my voice now, her own voice sharpened. "What's amiss? If Annabel Renwick has—"

"No!" I said. "I can manage her malice." I inhaled a long, sustaining breath of sweet baby-scent from my niece's warm neck. Then I jiggled her around in my arms so she could view the rest of the room as I forced a smile for her mother. "I don't need you or Jonathan to protect me from her anymore, I promise."

"Hmm." Amy settled into the chair across from my desk. "What is it, then?"

"Don't you have a daughter of your own to worry about? You needn't—"

"*Cassandra.*" Her brown eyes narrowed. Her long brown fingers tapped ominously against my desk. "Don't waste my time!"

"Oh, fine!" I blew out a sigh. "I just..."

What was there to say? The raw truth was that I wouldn't take back any of my choices even if I could. What exactly did *that* make me as a sister, as a wife, and as a woman in our world?

I said, abruptly, "Wrexham made me promise not to give up this school for him."

"Well, I should certainly think not!" She let out a startled laugh. "After all the work you've put into it..."

"All the work *we've* put into it," I corrected her. "That's..." I stopped and took a deep breath.

Amy cocked her head to one side, expectantly.

But there were no words to express exactly how I felt, so I dropped my gaze to where baby Miranda clung to my right forefinger with one tiny fist. I let out my breath in a helpless sigh. "You do know how much I love you both, don't you?"

"Mm," said Amy thoughtfully. "And?"

I shrugged, and Miranda let out a gurgle of delight at the inadvertent bounce. "I just...don't want to ruin her prospects." I brushed my cheek gently against Miranda's hair. "That's all."

"A-*ha*!" said my sister-in-law, and straightened in her seat. "You've been talking to Honoria. *That's* what's sparked all this!"

I winced. "You really needn't—"

"Oh, I can speak her name perfectly well," said Amy, "whether or not she deigns to speak to *me* anymore. But if she's been threatening my daughter through you—!"

"Not specifically," I said hastily. "Only in the general sense of all the young women in Angland now doomed to lose their futures and end up locked up by their husbands and kept voiceless forever, only because I opened this school. *You* know."

"I certainly do." Amy settled back in her seat. "Trust me, I've heard that speech from her before."

I eyed her warily. "But it didn't stop you from supporting me?"

Everyone in the nation seemed in unanimous agreement that my own motivations could only be selfish, no matter how they felt to me—but no one could *ever* claim such a thing about Amy. My sister-in-law cared fiercely and undeniably for the good of other people. That was the motivation that had driven her entire career, from her fight to allow more refugees from the continental wars into Angland to the speech she'd given the Boudiccate only three months ago on the need for more common land in the countryside. Yes, she was loyal to our family above all, but still...

"Oh, Cassandra," said Amy, "have you never paid *any* attention to the politics of the Boudiccate? Yes, Honoria and I were friends for many, many years, but that hardly means that we've always—or even usually—been in agreement."

"I do think," I said cautiously, "that Annabel Renwick is holding some sort of threat over her right now. Miss Fennell thinks so, too. So that might explain—"

"Oh, Honoria doesn't need any special explanations for her feelings on *this* matter," said Amy briskly. "When it comes to any question of change, you must know she's one of the most conservative members of the Boudiccate and always has been, despite all the forward-looking fashions that she wears. She cares deeply and sincerely for the safety of Angland and for our rights as women—and I respect her passion on both subjects—but that does *not* make her the final authority on what may or may not happen in the future."

She shook her head, reaching across the desk to scoop Miranda back from me as my niece's gurgles turned into wordless grumbles about the unforgivable lack of milk to be found on my chest. Two months ago, both Amy and I would have panicked at her sudden distress; now, after nine weeks of practice, Amy casually unbuttoned her bodice and attached her daughter without even glancing away from my face.

"*Trust me*," she said firmly. "If I thought Thornfell would be the downfall of our nation, I would have told you so in no uncertain terms. *Did* I?"

"No," I said, "but you might have privately felt—"

"I didn't enter politics," said Amy, "with the aim of keeping Angland exactly as it always has been. I came to make changes for the better, and *that* is what we're doing right now, here at Thornfell."

She waved her free hand sweepingly at the room around us as her daughter nursed. "Yes, *of course* the current situation is exceedingly comfortable for women like Honoria and I, who were born into just the right families and the right positions for what we wished to do with our lives. But what about you? What about your brother? And what about every man or woman in the nation who grew up without all of your manifold advantages?"

She shook her head vigorously as she adjusted Miranda's position. "It's not good enough for things to be easy for us. They have to be fair for *everyone* in Angland. And no, we won't achieve true parity this year, with this particular school, or even in our own lifetimes. But we *must* do what we can to move forward as a nation—and give our descendants the chance to do *better*."

"You wild radical, you!" I couldn't help smiling as I gazed across the desk at my sister-in-law, taking in the ferocity and love that emanated from her in equal measure as she cradled my niece in her arms. "Has anyone in the Boudiccate ever realized what a rebel you truly are at heart?"

"Not until this year, apparently." Her own smile was

rueful. "But if I gave up my principles and my family only to achieve personal power for myself...then what kind of politician would that make me?"

"Annabel Renwick's kind," I said. "Obviously! *She'd* give up anyone and anything for power...and she has, too." I sighed as I thought back to Miss Fennell's frozen expression the night before, under Annabel's insinuating pressure. "Is there anyone in the political realm whom she *isn't* either blackmailing or trying to blackmail?"

"She certainly enjoys being in control," Amy said judiciously. "And you must know this particular mission is personal for her. She never forgave your mother for sacking her; me for taking up her former position; or Jonathan for persuading your mother to drop her in the first place."

"*Or* me," I finished heavily, "for being my mother's daughter without wanting the legacy that came with it. Besides, I was the real reason she was sacked, and she knows it."

"Regardless..." Amy shrugged. "We can safely say that she would be delighted to strike a blow to our whole family. The only question now is: how do we stop the other members of the inspection team from voting with her?"

After the two lectures I'd endured in the past twenty-four hours, it wasn't a particularly hopeful question.

I tapped my quill pen restlessly against my notes as I thought, leaving new droplets of green ink across the pages. "I would say that you should talk to Honoria," I said, "but as she's been blackmailed into cutting you off completely... What *do* you think Annabel is holding over her, anyway? She doesn't have any private scandals that you know of, does she?"

Amy's face tightened. "If she did, it would have happened during her time as ambassadress to the Elven court, years ago. I always wondered..." She paused, pursing her lips, then gave her head a sharp shake. "*No*. I won't gossip about her private history, even if she isn't speaking to me at the moment. It wouldn't be kind or fair to our old friendship—and unlike Annabel, we *don't* engage in personal blackmail to achieve our ends."

"I suppose not," I said glumly, "although if there were anything we could hold over *Annabel*..." At Amy's meaningful look, I groaned and tossed down my pen. "Oh, come now! You can't blame me for wanting to serve her some of her own medicine."

"Blackmail," said Amy primly, "is highly illegal. *Which means*, of course..." Her eyes narrowed in thought. "If we could only prove, without a doubt, that she *is* blackmailing anyone for her own political gain, then the Boudiccate would be forced to dismiss her. They wouldn't have any choice—in fact, she'd be lucky to escape a prison sentence. But in order to prove that case—"

"We'd need someone to admit that they'd been blackmailed," I finished for her. "What politician would ever confess to such a thing?"

"Whoever it was would lose *her* career as well," Amy said. "Not only for whatever secrets she'd been blackmailed with in the first place but for the fact that she'd allowed blackmail to affect her political decisions."

"So it's useless," I concluded grimly.

"Is it?" Amy looked with unhidden satisfaction at baby Miranda, who had finally fallen fast asleep and flopped, apparently bonelessly, against her mother's chest, snoring softly. "I seem to recall," Amy murmured as she re-buttoned her bodice one-handed, "a certain young woman of my acquaintance being told *many* times—by some of the highest authorities in our nation!—that it was useless for any woman to dream of becoming a magician. And yet..."

"That's true enough." The weight of exhaustion pushed down on my shoulders, pulling my smile into a wry curve as I braced myself for the next great battle. "I never heard it from you, though. Not even in the very beginning."

"Of course not. I *know* you, Cassandra Harwood," said my sister-in-law drily. "Telling you that something is *impossible* is a guaranteed method to make you throw yourself at it with all your heart within a day."

"Ha!" I rolled my eyes at her. "As if you were any different? You're only more subtle about your methods."

"Which is why we work so well together." Amy smiled serenely as she rose from her chair, balancing my sleeping niece in her arms. "Now, if you'll excuse me—"

"Wait." As little as I wanted to bring up dark magic and forbidden fey altars with my innocent niece in the room, this conversation had been the reminder I needed: *no one* was more sharply observant than my sister-in-law. It would be foolish not to ask if she had seen that silver ring. "I wanted to—"

The door opened without a knock. "I'm sorry to interrupt you ladies," Miss Birch said, "but I thought you'd better know: that good-for-nothing weather wizard never showed up for the class he was meant to teach this morning. So the back courtyard's swarming with young ladies, all of them milling about without a thing to do—and those inspectors of yours are telling them *all* exactly what to think of it."

I HADN'T EVEN REALIZED I COULD RUN SO SWIFTLY THROUGH the green-and-bronze rooms of Thornfell. I emerged into the courtyard less than two minutes later, my pulse hammering against my throat, to find the time-weathered flagstones covered with pacing and fidgeting young women in various stages of irritation and distress—and Annabel Renwick's voice rising authoritatively above all of them.

"Of course one never likes to speak ill of such an old and well-respected family—"

"And so, *of course,* one would never be so crass as to do so, particularly in their own home," I finished firmly as I swept through the crowd at a far more dignified pace than I had used to reach it. Nothing could be done about the fact that my hair was mussed and my skin flushed and perspiring—but I kept my smile bright and my stride confident as I strode through my gathered students and pointedly focused on them rather than on my inspectors.

"I *do* beg your pardon for the inconvenience," I told them, "but unfortunately, Mr. Luton's message to me went astray. I was only just alerted to the crisis that called him away this morning."

"'Called him away?'" Lionel Westgate's eyebrows rose as he turned to me from where he'd been frowning in the direction of Luton's staff cottage. "But the man's right there, at home. He's simply refusing to answer his door."

Curse it! The bulk of the crowd stood between me and the small stone building, but when I slipped a quick glance in that direction, even I could make out a thin stream of smoke twisting and curling from its tall chimney.

I couldn't march over there to bang on the door myself in front of all of these onlookers—or tell Luton yet what I thought of his behavior, no matter how many viciously accurate phrases boiled within me. But...

"Called away *from his teaching duties,*" I said through my teeth. "The downside of having Angland's greatest weather wizard on-staff..." I almost gagged on the words, but I forced them out regardless. "...Is that he may sometimes be called upon to assist other wizards in their times of urgent need."

"Really?" Westgate's brow knotted. "Which ones?"

"I don't know the particulars of this case," I said tightly. "But he made his needs perfectly clear when I first hired him."

And I would make *my* feelings even more clear when I sacked him at the first possible opportunity. For now, though, I turned my back on Mr. Westgate to smile warmly at my students.

There was a wariness in more than one answering expression that I hadn't glimpsed in any of them before. Annabel's words had dealt their intended poison. I saw several of them dart questioning glances at her, looking for her assessment of the situation. I would have given a great deal to have Amy with me to defuse matters now, but I'd told her not to wake Miranda by coming with me.

She had trusted me to deal with this matter myself.

"I can't offer you a course in weather wizardry today," I said, "but we *can* take a brisk walk around the Aelfen Mere to clear our minds before we dive into our next lesson. As the breeze isn't too strong this morning, the lake might just be clear enough for us to glimpse the remnants of my father's famous ballroom underneath. Can anyone guess exactly where the greatest challenge lies in creating such an underwater structure through purely magical means?"

There was no simpler way to distract a magician of any level than to set them a magical puzzle. Even Mr. Westgate's brow crinkled in sudden, sharp interest, exactly as I'd hoped. Mother had never allowed him to read Father's groundbreaking spell—a gift to her on their wedding day—

despite all of his increasingly crotchety demands to view the particulars after Father's death.

But he wasn't too distracted by that question now to cast a final, speculative look backward as we all started up the hill toward Harwood House and the Aelfen Mere beyond, with Annabel and Lady Cosgrave murmuring ominously to each other at the back of our rustling group.

I'd wager anything that Mr. Westgate would be making a trip back to young Luton's cottage later that day to interrogate my wayward staff member himself. I would simply have to terrify Luton into good behavior beforehand. That part, I might actually enjoy.

But when I cast a vengeful look back at the cottage from the top of the hill, an unexpected sight stopped my breath.

I'd passed that cottage fifty times or more in the last few weeks. I knew it from every angle, and I could swear that no ivy or other spreading plant had ever come within ten feet of its sturdy stone walls since my new gardener had beaten back the woods' overgrowth. It should have been a plain gold block, neat and uniform on every side.

But from this angle, I could just catch a glimpse of the wall that faced the woods...and it was now colored a deep, dark green. *Something* was covering all those stones—something that hadn't been there the evening before, when I'd walked outside with Lionel Westgate.

Nothing could grow that quickly—nothing natural, at least. At the sight of that rich green, my stomach gave a convulsive lurch and my throat tightened uncontrollably...because it was a shade that I knew all too well.

It was exactly the color that had haunted my dreams every night for the past week and a half.

"Miss Harwood?" Miss Rao—a tall, elegant nineteen-year-old with light brown skin, a fashionable burgundy gown, and elaborately arranged, glossy black hair—spoke beside me, frowning. "Is something amiss?"

"I...beg your pardon?" With a blink, I forced myself back into the present moment—where I found myself surrounded by my entire, waiting class and inspectors.

How long had I stood, staring, silent, and unmoving? From the smirk on Annabel Renwick's face, I knew the answer had to be: *too long*.

"Forgive me!" I said hastily to the group as a whole. "I was only...thinking through an opportunity for our next lesson."

"Oh?" Annabel raised one mocking eyebrow. "Do enlighten us, please."

"I'm afraid you'll have to simply wait and see." Shaking out my skirts, I stalked forward. "There's no more time to be lost if we don't want to fall behind with our schedule for the day!"

"Any *further* behind, she means," muttered a low voice behind me. I didn't recognize the speaker—but then, it hardly mattered. Whoever she was, she could only be saying what everyone else thought by that point.

If I didn't want my new students to lose all faith in me and my curriculum, I had to focus on making our next few hours of lessons as challenging and satisfactory as possible...

But all that I could see before me as I strode up the graveled pathway toward my family's ancestral home was that poisonously familiar hint of deep, dark green that I'd glimpsed on Mr. Luton's cottage, just where it looked out onto the woods full of fey magic...

And I knew I wouldn't be able to concentrate on any other problem, no matter how vital, until I found a way to inspect it for myself.

9

B y the time my final morning session ended, I was ready to burst from my skin with impatience. I'd always known it would be a significant challenge to take on all the teaching at my own school apart from weather wizardry. At the Great Library, each lecturer had sole responsibility for only one or two classes per term; here, I was doing the work of at least three people, as no other magician would anger the Great Library by accepting a teaching post here.

Still, I'd never anticipated how it would feel to *know* there was a creeping menace encroaching on my property without being able to excuse myself and let anyone else take charge for the space of a single lesson.

It would have helped, of course, if my own solitary staff member had been available to assist me...but the more time that passed, the more that a new, piercing worry grew at the back of my mind, like thorny vines unfurling and stretching themselves luxuriantly.

Young Luton was more than stubborn enough not to answer his door when he was absorbed in a magical challenge; I'd experienced that scenario myself when I'd been forced to interrupt him in the midst of last winter's house party. But still...

What if he *hadn't* been immersed in work and stubbornly refusing to emerge for his lesson?

What if, instead, he hadn't been able to?

"You'll find a delicious luncheon from Miss Birch in the dining room," I said at the end of the morning's final lesson, "and I'll see you all at one o'clock."

There! Without waiting for any of the many questions sure to follow from our final exercise, I brushed off my hands and headed swiftly for the door.

"Miss Harwood?"

"Miss Harwood!"

"Aren't you joining us for our meal, Cassandra?" asked Lady Cosgrave.

"Not today." I forced a tight smile for the class's sake as I threw the door open. "But I do hope you'll all enjoy it!"

I whisked my way through the next room, walking quickly, until I was well out of sight...and then I ran.

I should never have let myself wait so long.

As I hurried through Thornfell's small back door, I peered past the gardens toward Luton's cottage and the vast woods beyond—and let out a heartfelt curse. Wicked green, leafy tendrils curled around both sides of the cottage now.

I couldn't see the thorns from here. But I knew they must be there, waiting. I'd seen those vines far too many times in my dreams not to recognize them in reality.

Heedless of any potential observers, I picked up my skirts and tore through the garden pathways like the wild, irrepressible girl I'd once been.

Too late, too late... The words drummed in my ears.

I rounded the final hedge and leapt onto the graveled

pathway that circled around Luton's staff cottage, ignoring the closed front door and curtained windows that faced me. Sharp stones bit through the thin soles of my ornamental silk slippers, which had already been worn thin by my unexpected hike earlier.

I thudded to a halt just past the cottage, panting.

Those vines were *everywhere*!

A slithering, thorn-studded, leafy chain had stretched from the woods beyond, bypassing all of the tall trees around it to reach purposefully for the cottage, where it split into a mass of writhing green vines. They'd already wrapped themselves around the facing wall and over the glass windows, too, blocking them in entirely.

They were exactly the type of vines that had swarmed around me, smothering me in my dreams every night for the past week and a half...and before my eyes now, they rustled harder, bunching together at the edges and then suddenly shooting forward, stretching themselves even further along the sides of the house and anchoring themselves at each new step with their sharp, predatory green thorns.

A convulsive shudder wracked my body. I remembered exactly how those thorns had felt in my dreams, piercing my skin as I'd struggled in vain to break free.

Then, last night, piercing Wrexham's throat before my eyes...

I couldn't let my thoughts rest on that image. Not now. I had a different gentleman to save.

Tearing myself free from my paralysis, I hastened back around the cottage before it could be surrounded completely.

The front door was locked. *Curse it!* We were in the middle of nowhere, as Luton had pointed out only yesterday. What burglars did he imagine might threaten his precious belongings?

"Luton!" I bellowed as I banged on the door. "Answer me, damn it! *Now*!"

"Is there a problem, Miss Harwood?" Mr. Westgate called out behind me.

I tipped my head against the wooden door for one brief but intense moment of anguish. Then I straightened and braced my shoulders. "Yes," I said, "there is."

I would do nearly anything to protect my fragile new school...but I would *not* sacrifice anyone else to my dreams.

...Or to my nightmares, at the present moment.

I stepped back, gesturing toward the closest wall of the cottage as Westgate crossed the final pathway from the gardens. He was moving at a brisk walk—but he came to a halt, eyebrows flying upward, as the leafy vines rustled and shot once more across the stones, gaining themselves another half a foot of territory.

"A radical new form of gardening, Miss Harwood?" he asked drily.

"Ha." I wouldn't let myself be baited. Not now. "Would you open this door for me, please? Mr. Luton still isn't answering, and I'd like to know for certain if he's in there."

"I did think that earlier story unlikely." Westgate gave a *harrumph* of amusement. "The idea of any mage voluntarily inviting Gregory Luton to lord it over them *yet again*..." Shaking his head, he closed his eyes...and then stepped back. "Unfortunately, I'll need another day or two before I can summon even the smallest of spells. We'll need to do this the old-fashioned way."

"The—?"

He lunged forward, shoulder-first, and slammed into the wooden door. It shuddered in its frame.

"Ah," I said. "*That* old-fashioned way."

It took only four hard blows to make the wood splinter —which meant that clearly, the staff cottage needed far more thorough a refurbishing than I'd realized. I would solve that problem later. For now, I reached through the ragged hole, ignoring the sharp shards of wood that scraped at my arm like claws, and I turned the inner lock myself.

"Luton!" I shouted. "We're coming in!"

No response greeted me. All I heard, when I strained, was the sound of rustling from the ivy several feet away.

Oh, Boudicca. I had killed him! When I'd turned away earlier rather than investigating; when I'd continued to teach my classes instead of tossing everything aside to save him...

"Well, Miss Harwood?" Westgate said. "*Are* we entering? Or did I bruise my shoulder purely for your entertainment? I'm not as young as I once was, you know."

I yanked my arm free and pushed the door wide open. "Of course," I said through numb lips. "We must find him, no matter what it takes."

...And then we'd have to inform his aunt, the Boudiccate's inspectors, *and* my students that I had failed to keep anyone on this estate safe after all.

At least there wasn't too much space to search. I took in the ground floor—parlor, garderobe, and kitchen—in six hasty strides, while Mr. Westgate's steady footsteps sounded on the stairs. Apart from the sheer number of books, papers, and half-drunk cups of tea that had accumulated atop the carpets during young Luton's single day of residence, there was nothing remarkable to be seen.

"No sign of him here," Westgate called down the stairs, "but his clothes and suitcases are still in his room."

"And his books and notes are down here," I called back.

It was the detail I needed to wrest my mind back into working order, despite the panic shrieking in my ears. If I thought of this *not* as the downfall of my school and a moment of shame that would haunt me forever, but simply as a challenging puzzle to be solved...

Think, Harwood. It was Wrexham's voice that I imagined, steadying me as always.

What did I actually know? Luton's clothes and books were here—so he hadn't simply marched away from Thornfell in a huff, seething over my inadequate attention to his 'requirements.' That would have been bad enough, given our ongoing Boudiccate inspection. But any other possibility...

Rustling sounded outside the window, and my spine tightened, ribs squeezing reflexively inward as if I were trapped in my dreams once more, being inexorably compressed. How much time did we have before those vines stretched themselves across the door? With neither Westgate nor I capable of casting spells at the moment, I didn't savor the idea of wrestling sharp thorns bare-handed.

That being said...

I gave a second, sharper look around the parlor where I stood. There were no footprints on the scattered papers, and none of the tea cups had been spilled—which was a genuine accomplishment, considering how many were scattered so close about the floor.

The clear window in this room faced up toward Thornfell, a perfectly comforting sight; I set my jaw and hurried back into the kitchen that faced the far more forbidding woods. Its murky light made me feel slightly ill as the rustling vines wrapped around and around the glass, like smothering serpents pressing against it...

But not one of them had managed yet to reach inside. The window was still safely shut and latched.

Footsteps sounded on the staircase behind me. Still frowning at those vine-covered windows, I asked, "Did you see any signs of a struggle upstairs?"

"None." Westgate stepped into the kitchen with me. "And the windows are all fully closed."

I turned around, my gaze sweeping the floor one more time. "So he hasn't been kidnapped from this house." I might roll my eyes at Luton's oft-repeated estimation of his own abilities, but even the weakest graduate of the Great Library must still have left visible signs of self-defense in the wake of any such attack.

Moreover, those vines, ominous though they appeared, certainly weren't doing anything to attack us at the moment. I didn't see how they could, without any gaps to wriggle through...

...Except, of course, for the splintered front door that Westgate and I had left hanging wide open.

Damnation! I snatched up a sharp knife from the sideboard and strode for the door without a second thought. "We need to get out. *Quickly.*"

"Hmm," said Westgate, and followed me.

Vines rustled at both sides of the doorway now, weaving back and forth at the edges like hunting dogs nosing for a scent. The unnatural sense of *awareness* in those movements sent dread shooting down my spine. Against my will, I rocked to a halt a full foot away as dark memories came screaming back, my breath choking in my throat.

Every night, over and over again...

It was broad daylight, and I stood on Harwood land, responsible for everyone I'd brought here. Firming my grip on the wooden handle of the knife, I forced breath through my chest and stepped directly between those questing thorns.

"Miss Harwood!" Westgate barked a warning just as vines shot toward me from both directions.

I threw myself forward, cold sweat drenching my skin...

...And landed hard on the gravel path beyond the house, my slippers skidding across the tiny stones. Clutching my knife, I spun around—and let out a half-laugh of disbelief. The attacking vines had collided behind me. Thorns spiked into each other's green flesh as they tangled and struggled to rip themselves free.

Mr. Westgate ducked swiftly underneath the writhing green knot, one hand shielding his grizzled head, and emerged unscathed with a silver pocketknife revealed between his dark fingers. He slipped it back into his waistcoat as he joined me, turning to study the writhing mass from a safe distance.

"So," he said. "They're instinctive, but not intelligent."

I frowned, following his gaze. The vines flailed violently against each other, tangling more and more with every movement.

"Oh," I breathed, "I do see. They can't communicate with each other." If they could, they would have freed themselves already, working together. Instead, they continued to attack each other every bit as aggressively—and automatically—as they'd aimed themselves at me when I'd stepped between them.

"And yet, they all came here at once—quite purposefully." Westgate's gaze shifted to the trees that loomed beyond the cottage, the woods from which that original cord of vines had come. "Unless this sort of visitation is a regular occurrence on your family's estate?"

I let out an impatient huff of air. "Do you think I'd have settled a staff member here if that was the case?"

"Hmm." His tone made my back teeth grind together.

Perhaps, in his eyes, I did seem capable of even that degree of irresponsibility in service to my own selfish whims. But—for better or for worse—he was the only trained magician within reach, and I had a missing staff member to recover. I hadn't the privilege of stalking off in offense.

"We must find Luton before anything else," I said evenly, my fingernails biting into my palms. "Even if he's only wandered off on his own, we can't leave him to be attacked by those things once he returns."

"Yes," said Westgate, "I have quite a few questions I'd like to ask young Luton. I'd particularly like to know what, exactly, he has been doing in this cottage, to bring about this unexpected visit from the local wildlife."

"Ah." I winced. Of course that would be Westgate's natural first assumption—but it was time, undeniably, to reveal what Miss Banks and Miss Fennell had discovered in the library last night, no matter what dangers that revelation might bring to my school. "I'm not certain it was Luton's fault, actually. I—"

"*Miss* Harwood!" Westgate expelled a heavy sigh of exasperation as he turned away from the ivy-wrapped cottage. "I can see that you are loyal to your staff members, no matter how rash your hiring decisions may have been. That loyalty does you credit, I admit. But right now, I have only one question for you to answer: *did* you take any time to study Luton's notes when you came across them in that cottage?"

He shook his head even as I opened my mouth to respond. "You did *say* you had spotted them in the parlor, didn't you?"

"They were scattered underfoot," I said impatiently. "I didn't take the time to read them, but—"

"Then," said Mr. Westgate, "the next step is to find our way back inside to examine them, *without* being trapped there afterward. Unfortunately, I can't cast any spells myself to ease our passage, so I'll be off now to summon one of my officers of magic rather than wasting any time on pointless debate, if you please. Keep your young ladies away from Luton's mess while I'm gone, and I'll see to the rest, as usual."

"*Mr. Westgate.*" I forced my voice under control. "If you'll only take a moment to listen—"

He let out a brusque half-laugh. "Like every other member of your family, you've always believed that your own opinions take priority in all circumstances. But I work for the nation, *not* for you, Miss Harwood—and as we both know, I've a great deal more experience with this sort of magical crisis than you. So, if you'll excuse me—"

"No," I snapped, "I will not! I am *trying to tell you*—"

But he was already jogging away in long, ground-eating lopes. I couldn't possibly catch up, and if I let out the scream of fury that was boiling up my throat right now, he would take it as proof of everything he'd ever said about me.

I grabbed my hair with both hands and yanked hard to relieve my feelings, dislodging half a dozen pins in the process. The sharp pain hurt, but it also cleared my senses.

With my chignon hopelessly unraveling around my shoulders, I spun around and strode for the house, skirts swishing purposefully around my legs.

It was time to rewrite this afternoon's lesson plans.

I could see increased wariness in many of my students' eyes when they assembled once again after lunch. Whatever poison Annabel had been dripping into all of their ears during the meal had apparently had an effect.

"Ladies!" Ignoring the tension in the room, I clapped my hands briskly together. The last of my students, Miss Stewart, stepped into the parlor, followed by the Boudiccate's beautifully-attired trio of politicians. Westgate, of course, was nowhere to be seen; he'd driven one of my sister-in-law's gigs to the nearest estate owned by another magician, some six and a half miles from Harwood House. He wouldn't be back for at least another hour.

I, however, had magicians right here in front of me. Westgate might not think them worth training, but I knew exactly how much potential every young woman in this room carried. All they needed was direction.

"For our next lesson," I said, "we shall take on a practical challenge, rather than any theoretical work. Please note, though, that this *will* involve working together at every step. Not one of you has yet developed the strength to work this spell alone." I swept the room with a gimlet gaze worthy of my own mother at her most severe. "This is *not* a moment to attempt to prove your skills by leaping ahead of the rest of the class. When it comes to magic, you must build your strength gradually, as you would any other muscle, or risk breaking it irreparably."

"As she would know," Annabel murmured from the back of the room.

I didn't even pretend not to hear her. "Exactly so," I said grimly. "That is why I will *not* allow any of my students to risk their own powers or safety in my school. Understood?"

I myself had been—notoriously—rash enough, strong enough and fortunate enough to survive any number of risky magical gambles across the years, all for the sake of proving my own powers to a skeptical and hostile world...until that final gamble, last year, when my luck had run out. That last spell had nearly killed me—and although I had survived it in the end, multiple experts had confirmed that if I ever drew on my shattered magical resources to cast even the simplest and most trivial of spells, the act would kill me instantly.

I would fight to the death to keep any girl I taught from ever sharing my own final magical experience.

I could see the frustration in many of their faces now, but a reluctant chorus of acceptance rippled around the two half-circles of chairs.

"In that case...." I stepped aside to reveal the large white basin of water that sat upon the high table at the front of the room. "I'd like two volunteers to begin with, please."

"Pardon me, Miss Harwood." Lady Cosgrave's voice was sharp-edged as she tapped the commonplace book in her hand, ignoring the hands of all of my students shooting up before her. "Doesn't this mark a significant alteration from the syllabus that you presented to your students last night?"

"Yes," I said. "Now, for my first—"

"So you're making a *second* significant change already?" Her voice carried easily through the room, lilting with just the right amount of disbelief to be persuasive. "After Mr. Luton's...*surprising* non-appearance this morning?"

I stretched my lips into a thin smile. "How serendipitous that you should mention him now," I said, "because Mr. Luton himself is to be the object of our spell."

A rustle of interest swept through my students, and I nodded. "He couldn't teach you this morning, but you will see him now *if* you can, together, cast a successful scrying spell. This will be a test of your memory, your powers of concentration, and your ability to work with your class-mates, blending your powers together into a whole."

"And has Mr. Luton volunteered to be the object of this spell?" Annabel inquired idly from her seat. "Or is this simply a discourteous jest that you're playing on a defense-less member of your staff?"

"Mrs. Renwick. *And* Lady Cosgrave." I looked pointedly from one of them to the other. "Correct me if I am mistaken, but you were intended to be unbiased *observers* of these lessons, were you not? Rather than active participants—or hindrants to them?"

"Well!" Lady Cosgrave's eyes flashed. "If you think—"

"I am *aware*," I snapped, "that both of you would prefer my students to remain uninstructed in their magical abili-ties. You have both made your feelings on the matter *quite* clear. Therefore, it can only serve your purposes to interrupt my lessons and subvert my students' faith in me during these few days that I've been granted for your inspection. But"—I held up one hand to still any further objections—"I *will not* leave any of these young women without a foundation for their own further studies, no matter how many underhanded angles of attack you may pursue against my school."

My gaze landed meaningfully on Annabel's face with my final words. She frowned warily in response, compressing her lips together.

Was she thinking of that sinister fey altar in the library? She must have known I would suspect her as soon as it was discovered. Not only was she the least trustworthy of our visitors, she was also the only one who had lived before on this estate, with more than enough opportunity to learn about our local fey traditions. I would have loved to press her further now, but with every minute that passed, I could feel those ominous, *directed* green vines wrapping ever tighter around Luton's house...and possibly even starting toward Thornfell itself.

Lady Cosgrave gave an impatient huff and began to scribble rapid notes in her commonplace book—an outline, no doubt, for the excuses she would give when she inevitably voted to close Thornfell down. I ignored the busy scratching of pencil against paper and turned back to my wide-eyed students. "Miss Banks and Miss Stewart, if you please. I'll direct both of you through it at first, before the rest of the class splits into their own pairs."

Miss Banks had studied magic before she came here, using the books that I had lent her, and Miss Stewart—the final student without an alibi for last night's doings—was also the only student who had been notably excited to study weather wizardry with Gregory Luton himself. None of my students knew him personally yet, but she, at least, knew *of* him—and that, I hoped, might add just a touch of personal connection to seal the scry.

It was maddening not to be able to perform the scrying spell myself and race to save Luton immediately...but this many months after my accident, I refused to allow bitter helplessness to overwhelm me any longer. Taking a deep breath, I accepted it...and let it go.

"Now," I said as my students moved into position on either side of the table, "join hands, look into each other's eyes, speak these words, and *focus*."

It was easy for them to repeat the words of the spell I recited for them next—but to focus, sincerely and wholly, in that moment was a challenge. There was an unavoidable jolt of startlement, of course, whenever one looked directly into another person's eyes for the first time. For two magician's magics to connect, that look could be nothing so simple as a brief or neutral glance. Shields had to be dropped on both sides for a true connection to be made.

Our magic came from the rawest, most vulnerable parts of ourselves. We had to open ourselves completely in order to share it.

And then, when two magics met and joined, guided by the simple words of that spell...

I had been talking, calmly and steadily, to my students throughout the process, but I had to clench my hands to hold back a full-body shiver as vivid memories suddenly splashed across me: the first time I had learned to do this myself, in a stuffy, windowless classroom at the Great Library, wearing my long black student robes and looking—inevitably—up into Wrexham's dark eyes.

I looked at him; he looked at me. It had been that way ever since I'd first arrived and awareness had sparked wildly between us. Everything we did, we did to show off to each other. We were acknowledged rivals in every class. We were intense and combative friends outside.

But that day, under the droning instruction of our professor, we were forced, at long last, to drop every one of our clever, protective barriers as we met each other's gazes. None of our emotions could be safely hidden any longer.

And the raw hunger that I'd seen in his eyes then, as my magic burst free and merged with his...

Heat washed through me at the memory, tingling and irrepressible—and *entirely* inappropriate. I gave my head a quick, sharp shake. This was *not* a recollection to indulge in whilst teaching!

Fortunately for the heat levels in our own classroom, Miss Banks and Miss Stewart shared no such personal history as Wrexham and I had. There was some awkwardness and shuffling of feet as their gazes connected, but none of the crackling emotional tension of my own experience. It took more than a few minutes before they managed to relax, slow their breathing, and truly focus in unison, but once they did—

Ah! Their magics connected with a burst of power that sent prickling energy through the room and made every hair on my arms stand on end.

Indrawn breaths sounded from every watching student —and when I glanced across the semicircles of chairs, holding up one hand for silence, I was startled to find the ever-imperturbable Miss Fennell staring at her secret fiancée with shockingly naked intensity. I wouldn't have expected her to know what that sudden shift in air pressure meant—but then, perhaps what she was reacting to was the sight of Miss Banks leaning forward, lost in her classmate's gaze...for Miss Stewart, it had to be said, was remarkably attractive, with curling auburn hair, full lips, and a mischievous sparkle to her eyes.

I gave my two students a full minute to adjust to their

new fusion, keeping a minatory gaze on their audience to ensure that not a single sound could distract either of them. That magical melding couldn't help but feel astonishingly intimate and exhilarating, no matter who the partner might be; paired with one's worst enemy, one would still thrill to sense that sudden doubled well of magical strength, making anything—anything!—seem possible.

It was a feeling I missed horribly...but I couldn't blame Miss Fennell if she felt an ignoble pang or two as she watched it happen. Knowing exactly how intimate that magical union felt, I shouldn't care to watch Wrexham pair with anyone else, either, for all that I knew better than to rationally mind it.

I should have liked to give my students more time to absorb the sensation, but the thought of those wicked, growing vines was a constant irritation at the back of my mind. So, after a minute, I stepped closer to Miss Banks and Miss Stewart, keeping my voice low and soothing, the better not to jolt either of them into dropping the connection. "Look," I said, "down into the water, but don't let go of each other's magic. Feel it filling the air between you, tying you together into one force."

Moving as slowly as if the air had become thick liquid, they followed my directions, leaning over to look down with glazed eyes. The water in the white bowl between them rippled under their twinned breath, perfectly transparent.

"Think," I said, "of Mr. Luton. Recall every detail that you can, no matter how small or insignificant. It could be the shade of his hair, the sound of his voice, or the words he spoke in his introduction last night." *Or the way he sprawled in his chair afterward as if he owned the whole estate*, I thought uncharitably.

The water in the bowl was already swirling, colors

seeping in through the growing whirlpool. Green and gold and blue—*aha*! That was the blue of Gregory Luton's eyes...seen so close, as the vision settled into place, that his face filled the entire bowl, and the green and gold I'd glimpsed along the way were abandoned far outside the confines of the water.

Good God. Was Miss Stewart *really* only interested in Luton's weather wizardry? Because the vision summoned here, stemming from the most vivid impression plucked from either of the two women's memories...

Never mind. I would have a firm talk later with Miss Stewart about the inadvisability of being taken in by a pair of fine blue eyes, waving golden hair, and an impressively confident demeanor.

In the meantime, I kept my own voice pitched low as I murmured, "Well done, both of you. Now, let yourself fall back a bit. Let's see more than just his face, shall we? Hold onto your sense of him, but move away slowly...yes. *Just* like that. Perfect!" Water swirled again, reshaping itself within the bowl, and pride lit within my chest like a lantern, casting away the last shadows of frustration.

Yes, I could have cast this spell myself a year ago, with ease—but to watch my students discover the wonder of casting it together? And to see them do it so well on their first try? *That* was a gift beyond any measure.

I leaned forward to catch every detail of their vision as colors settled into place...and my jaw clicked shut as sudden outrage overwhelmed my pride.

Oh, *damn* the man!

That green did indeed come from vegetation, but not at all the kind I'd feared. Branches swayed around Luton's shoulders, heavy with lush green leaves that brushed gently against his skin as he frowned in thought, tapping one hand against his chin.

No vines were in sight; nothing compelled him to remain. He stood free and unhindered, without the slightest trace of fear or anxiety in his expression. After all the hours I'd spent panicking that he might be trapped, tortured or worse, *he*, apparently, had been ignoring his teaching duties to take a pleasant stroll in my family's woods—*exactly* as I'd warned him against on his arrival!

A fleck of blue formed in the corner of the vision, and I sucked in a breath, leaning closer. There, just in the corner of the vision...

"Are those *bluebells*?" Annabel inquired over my shoulder.

If there had been a wall nearby, I would have banged my head against it.

Gregory Luton had walked directly into the woods during bluebell season and hadn't even made any attempt to avoid them.

As if Annabel's words had been a summons, my seven watching students all leapt from their seats and crowded around us, bobbing up and down to peer over our assorted shoulders. Under other circumstances, I would have waved them back to preserve Miss Banks's and Miss Stewart's joint focus, but I was too busy battling down rage to trust my own voice at that moment.

He had *known* that we were under Boudiccate inspection. He'd known just how vital these few days would be for Thornfell—for every new dream I'd cherished since I'd lost my magic, and for every girl who deserved a magical future of her own.

Against my own better judgment, I had given him a chance to prove himself—the kind of chance I would have given anything to win after my own time at the Great Library—and as his thanks, he had quite possibly ruined my school's chances forever.

"Shall we—?" Miss Banks began.

I cut her off. "Excellent work, both of you." My voice shook with anger; I ignored the tell-tale wobble as I swept one hand firmly between my two scrying students. "You may sever the connection. *Now*."

"But—!" Miss Stewart began, even as the image fizzled in the bowl before her.

"I am very pleased with your first scrying attempt," I said, "and so will Mr. Luton be. He wasn't sure you'd be able to find him in that woods on your first attempt, especially if he stood so close to bluebells."

And here I was lying to my students...*again*! This was the second time I'd deceived them for Luton's sake. That knowledge burned into me like venom sizzling against the bright, open flower of Thornfell's potential. But with the Boudiccate's inspectors watching and waiting to pounce upon the slightest misstep...what choice did I have?

"Now," I said tightly through whirling, furious regret, "I believe it's time for our second attempt. Miss Hammersley, please? And Miss Rosenthal? I believe we'll attempt a different challenge this time. Perhaps...an object rather than a person. Do either of you have a suggestion? Perhaps a landmark you both know?"

My students obediently shifted places around the basin. Miss Hammersley and Miss Rosenthal bent their heads toward each other for a quick, whispered consultation. Miss Stewart and Miss Banks gave each other half-shy, half-laughing looks of victory. Miss Fennell's face returned to its previous cool mask, her gaze shuttered and enigmatic.

The vines from my nightmares had arrived in real life

and were smothering my staff cottage. The only weather wizard willing to teach at my school was merrily ignoring his responsibilities so he could take a nature walk around the most dangerous and infamous fey flowers in the nation, leaving me to face the Boudiccate's inspectors alone. And Annabel Renwick stood directly behind me, her breath on my neck, only waiting for me to make a single mistake that she could use to ruin me forever.

I drew a deep, steadying breath and forced myself to smile as my students looked to me for direction. "So," I said. "Let us continue with our lesson."

11

M r. Westgate did not reappear within an hour or two, as planned. Instead, a note arrived in his place, whisking into mid-air in the middle of my final lesson with a brief flare of magical energy that must have been borrowed from his host.

Have been called away on an urgent matter. Will return. Until then, keep your students well away from Luton's folly. – LW

I pressed my lips together and drew in a long breath through my nose.

Of course he hadn't bothered to talk with me before he'd left. *Of course* he hadn't been interested in anything *I* might have learned in the meantime...or in the *extremely* pertinent details from last night that I'd tried in vain to share with him earlier.

Luton's folly, indeed. Furious though I might be with Thornfell's soon-to-be-dismissed professor of weather wizardry, Luton was not the *only* arrogant male to be contributing heavily to today's chaos.

So much for last night's promise to Wrexham that I would get magical help from his supervisor if we needed it!

"Interesting news?" Lady Cosgrave inquired from her seat, her silver pencil hovering above her commonplace book.

"Only a note from Mr. Westgate." I folded the cream-colored paper and deposited it safely within a hidden pocket in my gown. "He's been called away, but he trusts we can manage without him."

"Yet another magician mysteriously called away on urgent business," murmured Annabel. "First Luton, now Westgate. Shall we expect you to disappear on us too, Cassandra? –Oh, wait. I'd actually forgotten for a moment." She smiled lushly. "You aren't *really* a magician yourself anymore, are you?"

It was becoming easier and easier not to rise to her bait. Keeping my expression blank, I looked past her to my students, who had paused in their work to observe the barbed byplay. "Has anyone finished yet?"

They all hastily bent back over their slates, on which they were each sketching out in chalk their own proposed steps for a new spell to summon light.

Calmly and steadily, I crossed the room and gave the bell-pull a light tug. When my housemaid appeared in the doorway a minute later, I mouthed the words *Miss Birch* to her while keeping my back carefully turned to our inspectors.

Ciara was a clever girl. She nodded and slipped away without asking any questions...and twenty minutes later, as the last of my students streamed out of the room to return to their own quarters before supper, Miss Birch stepped inside with her gaze uncharacteristically downcast and her hands clasped, looking as meek and unnoticeable as a stick in the woods. *Perfect*.

Annabel's gaze slipped straight past her. "Will we be seeing you at supper, Cassandra?" Lingering behind her co-inspectors in the doorway, she raised her eyebrows with faux-concern. "Or will you be too busy to share a meal with your students...again?"

"Oh, I'll be there," I said firmly, and gave her a look that added: *I know exactly what you're up to.*

It was an impressively ominous expression that I'd learned from my mother in my own rebellious youth—which made it even more unfortunate that my empty stomach chose to rumble a loud and undignified accompaniment at that very moment.

"Poor Cassandra." Annabel smirked. "So close to true power in so many ways...and yet, you never can *quite* pull it off, can you?"

Shaking her head, she sailed out of the room. I very nearly slammed the door behind her.

"Always a disappointment..." That had been her favorite phrase to sigh in my ear when I was a girl and no one else could hear us. Apparently, I hadn't yet outgrown the rage-filled reaction that that message inevitably inspired.

I *would not* disappoint everyone who relied upon me now, so I forced myself to shut the door with tooth-gritted care—and only then allowed myself to turn to my house-keeper. "So?" I said. "Have those vines come any closer?"

"Not yet." With the departure of the Boudiccate's inspectors, Miss Birch had unclasped her hands and resumed her usual sturdy pose, straight-backed and hard-elbowed, her hazel gaze piercing. "They're still busy tangling themselves around the cottage, so I set Brigid and some of her girls from the stable to build a good-sized fence around it. That should keep anyone from getting too close, for now."

"The higher the better," I said. "It should slow down the vines, too, if they change direction." I worried at my lower lip, envisioning those long, sharp thorns planting themselves firmly into slim wooden fencing as strong vines looped across it...or even tore it down. "Is there any chance that you could stop them from growing at all from now on? Or that you could change their direction and send them back into the woods?"

"Not without lifting protection from our house. I wrapped all my strength tight around Thornfell last night—that's why they had to settle for the cottage instead."

"I see." I sighed. "Well, there's no question which building is more vital to defend." As I was planning to dismiss Luton with *great* pleasure the moment he strolled back onto school grounds, there was no need to house him appropriately any longer. "The only question now is: how can we defeat whichever fey sent them after us?"

"Myself, I'd look to the human in this house who set that nasty, sneaking bargain to begin with." Miss Birch gave a derisive sniff. "However fine a lady she may be, she's only a visitor. Once we're rid of her, we should do well enough. None of the creatures in these woods ever caused any trouble for Harwoods until *she* came."

"Mmm..." A few weeks ago, I would have assented to that sentiment without a doubt. But all those vivid nightmares that I had experienced since moving into Thornfell—all those dreams of being smothered and pierced by vicious thorns from vines that had proven to be only too real, wielded by one of those wild fey in our woods...

What if all the official reasons for Thornfell's old abandonment were no more than face-saving excuses? So many gentlemen among my ancestors had bucked tradition by choosing to move back to Harwood House after their widowhoods, giving up, one after another, all of their claims to an honorable dower house in which they could be master. What if those choices *hadn't* arisen solely from family affection after all?

It would all suddenly make so much more sense...if, in fact, I wasn't the first Harwood to have had those suffocating nightmares forced upon me.

No such stories had been passed down in family lore— but then, as Lionel Westgate had pointed out, I was descended from a long line of men and women who'd all prided themselves on their personal strength. How many of my ancestors would have admitted to their brisk, powerful daughters—or, worse yet, to their magician sons-in-law— that they had been chased from their rightful home by bad dreams?

"Miss Harwood?" Miss Birch prompted.

But I was too furious to speak.

I loved Thornfell with all of my heart. Every weathered red brick and uneven golden stone in its eccentrically rambling exterior; every patch of green-and-bronze wall-paper and every brass lamp; every single inch of it, inside and out, was my home, the dream that I had built when my first dreams were shattered, the future I'd claimed for myself, for my students, and for Wrexham, too...should the Boudiccate ever allow him enough rest to enjoy it.

I wouldn't be driven away from it by *anyone*, no matter how powerful or ancient they might be. It didn't even matter, anymore, which of my human visitors had extended the blood-cast invitation that broke our old bargain with the fey and allowed those vines to finally manifest outside the woods. After so many endless nights spent tangled and tortured in my sleep, I knew one thing with certainty: whoever controlled them had been waiting a long time for this opportunity.

They were going to regret it.

"Keep up Thornfell's defenses," I said, "and have one of Brigid's girls keep an eye on that fencing—and on the woods beyond, as well. I want to know the moment that Professor Luton finally returns."

"Oh, *him*." She rolled her eyes. "Shall I have him sent to you when he finally comes creeping out of there?"

"Yes, please." I strode for the door. "And do let me know if you discover any clues about that ring from the altar." An identification sourced through fey magic might not be considered legal evidence in court, but I would dearly love to throw it in Annabel's sneering face anyway. "In the meantime, I have research to do before supper."

Until now, I'd focused on the human aspect of our attack. When it came to magical menaces, though, there was only one place to go. Thank goodness my family never let go of old books!

Amongst all of the dusty and outmoded volumes left piled in Thornfell's library to clear space in Harwood House's own library, I'd found all twelve of the leather-bound journals that had been hand-written by my most eccentric ancestor. Romulus Aeneas Harwood—born well over a century ago, in the days when the aristocracy of Angland had been fashionably fixated upon the Roman empire—was not one of those famous gentleman magicians whose portraits hung in the long gallery of Harwood House to impress awestruck visitors. My many-times-great-uncle had instead been discreetly forgotten by Anglish history outside the annals of our family...and our own family had never known quite what to do with him.

He had, of course, attended the Great Library, like every other male Harwood in our records until my own brother finally rebelled and broke that long tradition. However, rather than marrying a suitable politician, moving into her elegant house and building a magical career to the dizzying heights expected of any Harwood, he had inexplicably chosen to retire from public life at the age of twenty-two. Then he had—with quiet but utterly unbending determination—made Harwood House his home for the rest of his short life.

While his younger brother and older sisters had dazzled the world with their exploits, Romulus had spent nearly two decades, until his death from influenza at eight-and-thirty, sleeping in his childhood bedroom, taking daily walks around the estate, and filling volume after volume of his private journals with densely scribbled observations...that never left his room until his death finally revealed their existence to his baffled relatives.

As far as I knew, no one had ever read through all those volumes of detailed observations on every aspect of our estate. When I myself had come across them whilst sorting through Thornfell's old library, I'd flicked through the first page or so, shrugged, and placed them all into one of the wooden crates that held all the spare books that wouldn't aid my students' magical education. Like every Harwood before me, I'd seen those journals as necessary to preserve for the sake of family history...but hardly relevant to our current needs.

Now, though, I wished I'd kept them closer to hand. Ever since the grounds of our estate had first been drawn, the Harwoods and the fey within our woods had operated in an agreed-upon relationship of mutual respect and separation. We stayed out of the woods during bluebell season; they left us alone outside the woods. Beyond ceremonial offerings of milk and wine at the appropriate times of year—and, of course, my mother's annual Spring Equinox ball, which their ambassadress had always attended with a magnificent entourage—there had never been any compelling reason for us to investigate them further.

But if ever anyone in my family had had the time *and* opportunity to study the mysterious creatures in our woods, it would have had to be my most enigmatic and least famous ancestor.

It took fifteen minutes of digging through the piled crates in Thornfell's vast, stuffy attic before I found the one I needed. Dust motes floated through the air, lit only by the glow of my lantern, as I pulled out the stack of journals. There were twelve in all; none of them were slim, to say the least. I sighed as I gathered them all up in my arms.

This was yet another time when it would have been helpful to have a second committed professor on staff...but as it was, this would certainly be another sleepless night.

Exhaustion cascaded through me at the prospect. Even balancing all of these volumes in my arms on my way back down that ladder, whilst juggling both the lantern and my own long skirts, suddenly felt too much to contemplate. Expelling a weary sigh, I sagged back onto the dusty attic floor and pulled a random journal from the middle of the stack, holding it close to the lantern's golden glow to make out the cramped, old-fashioned scrawl inside.

Just for one or two minutes, I would let myself rest and see if I could find anything useful at random, before I went down to resume social jousting with our inspectors...then began a more thorough page-by-page search in the darkest hours of the night.

...are budding againe, theyre leaves salamander green and spreading in a pattern moste splendid and various...

The dusty, stuffy air settled around me like a thick, heavy blanket wrapping me in warm darkness. Yawning, I flipped to the next page to try again.

...sister's unending complaints, as she desired me to meet a certain Lady Montague "who mighte yette consider you even now if she only saw the magic you are capable of, Romulus." As if any other lady could compare to the bewitchments of my owne true beloved!

But I could hardly say as much to Octavia, so I was gladde to escape once again into the gardens, surrendering my breakfast meats to avoid any more tedious lectures on the subject of marriage...

His own true beloved? I blinked, sleepily absorbing that ancestral revelation. If Romulus really had been in love at that point in his life, his choice must have been shocking indeed to keep his sisters from leaping at the chance to hand him over to any bride who would willingly take him. An unmarried gentleman by the age of thirty was an embarrassment at best and a burden at worst—and those rules had been even stricter a century ago, like all of our other old ingrained prejudices. Who could have been so unsuitable a match that he couldn't even risk revealing her identity to his desperate relations by then? A stablegirl? An already-married woman?

Perhaps, if she had lived close by, that might explain...

Oh, never mind. My tired brain wandered only too easily down roads of distraction, but this wasn't the information I'd come searching for. Any gossipy side-paths down family history would have to wait for another night, when I could happily hand these journals over to my historian brother and enjoy a night of cozy speculation over glasses of sparkling elven wine. Perhaps Wrexham would even be able to join us, by then.

In the meantime...

I flipped through another dozen or so pages of detailed garden updates, heaved a final sigh, and closed the volume. The candle in my lantern was starting to gutter. My gown desperately needed a change before supper, and I had no idea how much time I had left to prepare. My hair was undoubtedly covered in dust. If I wanted to maintain any semblance of control over the meal, despite Annabel and Lady Cosgrave's finest conversational machinations...

The trapdoor popped open unexpectedly behind me, and I jolted hard at the sound, dropping the journal that I'd held to the dusty floor. As I scrambled around, a familiar, tousled brown head appeared through the opening. Jonathan pulled himself up into the attic a moment later, dressed in evening finery.

"What are you doing here?" Sighing, I gathered up our ancestor's journals once more. "Am I late for supper? Or—"

"Supper started half an hour ago," said my brother, "and apparently, Miss Fennell was hunting for you all over the house beforehand, but we have a more urgent problem at the moment." For once, there was no easy smile of reassurance on his face; a sigh of his own sent his broad shoulders sagging. "Amy sent me to find you as quickly as possible," he said. "Annabel Renwick is missing."

12

I didn't juggle everything after all. I grabbed the lantern, shoved the journals at Jonathan, and then lunged down the ladder with no care at all for the hem of my gown.

Annabel Renwick is missing.

"It makes no sense!" I snarled as I started for the staircase.

She was the one who had summoned that fey in the first place; I was certain of it. Who else would have had the sheer malice to wish it—*or* spent enough time on this estate to learn the local lore and think to make such a bargain in the first place? She was the only one who'd lived with us, filling Harwood House with her shadowy poison. She was the only one who hated me personally enough to risk her political standing, her social reputation, and even her freedom by summoning a fey to attack my school and ruin everything for me.

"Why would it attack *her*? That could break the entire bargain!"

"What bargain?" Jonathan demanded, long legs catching up with me. "What are you talking about?"

My older brother generally gave off an impression of easygoing charm no matter what the circumstances, but lines of tension marked his face now as he cradled our ancestor's journals in his arms. Exhaustion showed, too, in the dark shadows that spread beneath his blue eyes—marks of the sleep I knew he'd lost since his daughter's birth. The last thing he needed was to be drawn into yet another of my crises now...but I couldn't send him away now.

At any moment, I would face the wrath of Annabel's fellow inspectors. I had to arm myself with as much information as possible beforehand.

"Who discovered she was missing?" I asked, ignoring his question.

"She never came to supper. Of course, neither did you," Jonathan added with a wry glance, "but in *your* case, we all knew you must have got wrapped up in one of your projects, as usual, and not even noticed the passing of time."

"Hmmph." That...might not be entirely inaccurate, but it still made me sound too much like young Luton for my liking. I started down the stairs, moving quickly. "And then?"

"Well, no one would ever imagine that of our *dear* Annabel," said Jonathan with heavy irony, "as the only books she'd ever find that absorbing would be other people's private papers. Speaking of which, aren't these old Romulus's journals? He was meant to move into Thornfell himself, you know, if he hadn't caught that influenza that killed him only days beforehand."

"That is hardly—" I began.

But my brother had always been too easily distracted by history. "I thought I was the only one who'd ever bother to read these. What were you looking for, exactly? Clues to his mysterious, forbidden romance? Because I can tell you, I've read every single volume from cover to cover, and he never slipped up once when it came to keeping her secret. Up through the very last page, it's all meticulous observations about the plants and enigmatic sighing about how they could never truly be together."

"Never mind all of that!" I swung around the first curve in the wide staircase, the lantern dangling from my hand. "What happened *to Annabel*?"

"Ah. Well, Amy went to look for her when Lady Cosgrave started fussing."

Of course. Amy would have planned to manage that battle in private whilst delegating Jonathan to charm and distract the rest of the company. As a partnership, they'd often worked wonders in that fashion. In fact, if only the Boudiccate weren't too hidebound to admit it, my brother would have made an *excellent* husband for any politician. He didn't need any spell-cast magic to support Amy perfectly in all of her aims.

"When she came back, she told everyone else that Annabel was lying down with a sick headache and wished us to eat without her...but she whispered to me to come and find you without delay." Jonathan's voice was grim. "Apparently, Annabel wasn't anywhere to be found, but her bedroom was an utter shambles. Amy said it looked as if the woods had come inside."

Damnation! Blowing out the lantern, I lifted my skirts and broke into a run, dread pounding an inexorable beat in my ears.

No, no, please, no—

I flung open the door to Annabel's room.

The windows had been wrenched wide open. One hung half-detached, swinging in the evening breeze. Marks and dents had been punched into their wooden frame and into the wall below.

The bedcovers were tangled into a knotted mess. Perhaps Annabel had been lying down with a headache before supper after all. It was difficult to imagine her truly at rest—impossible to even conceive of her being vulnerable—but horribly familiar green leaves lay scattered across her bed, marked with unmistakable spots of blood.

The sight knocked every certainty out of my chest and left it hollow. I stood gaping, my fingers numb against the door handle.

How could this have happened?

Air hissed through Jonathan's teeth and ruffled the top of my head. "What the devil—?"

"We need Miss Birch. *Now*." I lurched inside to tug hard on the bell pull. "But don't let anyone else inside. I mean it!" As footsteps sounded on the staircase nearby, I pushed my brother's big body back and shut the door firmly between us. His sigh sounded through the wood, but a moment later, he addressed whoever was coming up the stairs in a perfectly cheerful whisper. "Just standing guard for Mrs. Renwick's nap! If you wouldn't mind keeping your voices down as you pass..."

Thank Boudicca for truly reliable men! Leaving the protection of the room to him, I strode quickly across the long, narrow floor, searching for clues on every surface. Of course I knew *what* had taken Annabel—I could visualize the whole event only too clearly, based on that desperate tangle of sheets and leaves on the bed, not to mention the trail of small, dark drops of blood between them and the open window.

But *why* had those vines taken her, of all people? And how had they travelled so far—and broken through Miss

Birch's guard—despite all the stablegirls set to watch for them by Luton's staff cottage?

I could barely stand to see those tiny, bloody drops. I stepped around them to peer out through the window, gripping the chipped windowsill with both hands...and then I saw another window hanging open just below.

Those vines hadn't had to grow all the way from Luton's cottage and around the bulky mass of Thornfell after all.

I was lunging through the bedroom door before I'd even had time to think, brushing past Jonathan's startled yelp as he jumped aside. "Downstairs," I snapped. "Quickly!"

We hurtled together down the staircase to the ground floor, making no attempts at silence anymore. I'd passed the point of caring for discretion the moment I'd seen that second pair of open windows below me and realized exactly which room they'd come from. That *anyone* would dare to use *my* library of magic as their setting for a forbidden fey summoning *again*—!

The dining room door flew open as we passed, students and inspectors spilling out with raised voices and wide eyes, but I ignored every question shouted after us.

Damnation! From this point onward, I was going to lock that library door whenever I wasn't there to guard it, no matter how important those books might be for my students' education.

Tonight, I was too late. The windows stood wide open to the evening breeze, which fluttered the long curtains as I exploded into the room. The culprit—whoever it had been —was long gone. Only green leaves, scattered across the carpet, along with marks I recognized on the windowsill itself, remained as taunting evidence of what had happened in the room I loved most, whilst I'd been buried in useless old family gossip three stories away, oblivious to what was transpiring below me.

Perhaps Westgate was right after all. I'd always understood *magic* on a bone-deep level, but when it came to looking after other people...

"What in the world is going on?" Lady Cosgrave demanded from the doorway behind me. Her silvering dark hair was piled high atop her head tonight and pinned into place by a truly magnificent ruby. A necklace of shining silver twined in intricate elven knots around her throat, and she sailed forward in her crimson fey-silk gown like a warship surging through a shoal of fishing boats as my students cleared hastily out of her path.

Amy stood just behind, one hand raised to her mouth as she took in the scope of the disaster. For once, my sister-in-law made no move to step forward and bring calm to the room; only too clearly, we were past any possibility of that. Her gaze shifted from the leaves and the open windows to me, her brown eyes wide and questioning.

The time for strategic misdirection had ended. I said, my voice pitched to reach the students who hovered outside the room, "Someone in this house has been bargaining with a wild fey to attack Thornfell. Now Mrs. Renwick has been taken."

"*Taken*?" Lady Cosgrave's eyebrows shot up as the crowd behind her dissolved into anxious gasps and whispers. "What do you mean, *taken*? To where, exactly?"

"The woods, I assume." There was nowhere else any wild fey could transport themselves so easily with an unwilling human companion. As this particular fey hadn't been thoughtful enough to drag Annabel inch-by-inch across the grounds for us to watch along their way, they could be hiding anywhere in those woods by now. I hadn't stepped past the tree line myself since bluebell season first began, and I'd never once stepped off the official woodland paths before the safety of Samhain any year, not even in my most rebellious youth.

Now, apparently, for the sake of my old childhood tormentor, that most immutable Harwood law—*Leave the fey to their secrets!*—was about to be broken for the first time...and yet again, my whole family might pay the price for my actions, if the rest of the fey in our woods took it as a final betrayal of our long agreement.

I clenched my jaw tight and bit out my words as Jonathan set down the piled journals and stepped up behind me in support. "We cannot rescue her without magical assistance. As soon as Mr. Westgate returns with one of his officers of magic—"

"Wait. She's been carried off to the *woods*?" Behind Lady Cosgrave, Miss Stewart blanched and clasped Miss Banks's bare forearm for support. "But Professor Luton, in our vision—"

"Indeed." Lady Cosgrave turned to give her cousin a meaningful look, and Miss Fennell swiftly averted her gaze from Miss Stewart's hand upon her secret fiancée's arm. "We did all witness Gregory Luton in those woods today, did we not? Standing directly by the *bluebells*."

"Oh, for—!" I forced myself to pause for a deep, sustaining breath, as Amy's warning gaze landed upon me. "Professor Luton had nothing to do with this matter, I assure you," I continued as steadily as I could. "In point of fact, I am almost certain that the true culprit—"

"Then what *was* he doing in those woods today? Especially after all of those dire warnings you issued last night?" She looked around the gathered company for support. "I wasn't the only one who heard them, was I? 'No one is to enter the woods on *any* pretext until the end of bluebell season, on threat of expulsion?'"

"That warning," I said, "was intended for *students*. Professor Luton is an established weather wizard, so—"

"Perhaps," said Amy, moving forward, "we should hear all of the facts before we start casting wild accusations in *any* direction. Cassandra?" Her tone and facial expression might appear as composed as usual in the midst of any political storm, but I knew Amy better than almost anyone, and what I glimpsed in the shadows of her gaze made the ground suddenly feel unbalanced beneath my feet. Could that be raw pain she was trying to hide? *Why*? What about this could have hurt her on such a personal level?

I wanted to turn to Jonathan for help, but she spoke again before I could. "What exactly *do* you know of what's been happening?" she asked me. "And how long has it been going on?"

Ohhh. I sucked in a breath as realization hit, sickeningly. *I* was the one who had hurt her. Damn it! "I wasn't keeping it a secret from you!" I said hastily. "We only discovered it late last night—"

"We?" said Lady Cosgrave sharply. "So there are *multiple* people in this house who knew of grave danger and intentionally kept it hidden from us?"

Her cousin's strong-boned face went stiller than ever. Safely outside Lady Cosgrave's line of sight, Miss Banks gave a tiny, frantic shake of her head.

Reluctantly, I released the safest truth available. "Wrexham was visiting me for the evening."

Amy's eyes widened. Behind me, I felt Jonathan shift position. But my focus was on Lady Cosgrave now, and I caught the exact moment that her lip curled with wry satisfaction. "What a pity," she murmured. "We had all understood that your husband, at least, was reliable in his work. But if he's been secretly traipsing about the nation for romantic assignations when he was meant to be fulfilling his official duties..." She shrugged. "I don't see how even I could defend him any longer to the others in the Boudiccate."

"You—?" My jaw dropped open. "Who *are* you, Honoria Cosgrave? Who have you allowed yourself to become?" The words ripped themselves from my chest; her familiar face turned even colder and more unreachable with every new word that I uttered. "You've known me since I was a child," I said desperately. "You *tried* to matchmake me and Wrexham last winter. I don't care how much you disapprove of my school. How can you possibly justify trying to ruin *him*?"

I shook my head in disbelief. "Whatever Annabel may be holding over you, *nothing* justifies what you're doing now."

If I hadn't known better, I would have thought she'd grown a full inch in her icy fury. "Believe it or not, Cassandra Harwood," Lady Cosgrave snapped, "you are *not* the only woman in this room with a mission to protect the vulnerable. And I would take *great care* with your personal insinuations about me and my colleagues! There are far worse fates possible for *anyone* than the loss of a mere magical appointment."

"Cassandra!" Amy hurried toward us, one hand outstretched. "This isn't the moment for recriminations or accusations. Perhaps if we all step outside and take a few minutes to calm ourselves before—"

"No!" I lurched away from her soothing touch for the first time in memory. Jonathan caught hold of my shoulders before I could slam into him, but I never looked away from Lady Cosgrave's frozen face. "I *cannot* let this go, not even for a moment! This isn't a political game to be played for points amongst colleagues. This is my husband's *life* and his career that you're threatening! Wrexham hasn't done anything wrong, and you know it. So long as he fulfills his professional duties to the Boudiccate—"

"I beg your pardon?" Lady Cosgrave let out a startled-sounding laugh. "Did Lionel Westgate not even mention why he had been called away in that message he sent you?"

"*What*?" I stared at her. "What are you talking about?"

"The private message *I* received from him an hour later, of course." She waved one hand impatiently, her ruby and topaz rings glinting in the fey-light. "I assumed he must have told you about it, too, and *that* was why you went and hid away from everyone for so long. My cousin went looking for you as soon as we received the message, but she couldn't find you anywhere. *I* might have chosen to discuss the matter with you myself after supper, but as you didn't bother to attend that meal, either..."

Jonathan's hands tightened around my shoulders, as if he feared I might lose control and strike her. Above my head, his voice sounded harsher than I had ever heard it. "I think we'd *all* like to know what that message said if it pertains to my brother-in-law, Lady Cosgrave."

Amy stepped up to close us into a tight circle of privacy, her back blocking the view of our onlookers. "Don't be cruel, Honoria," she murmured, too softly for anyone outside to overhear. "It's petty and beneath you, and you know it."

It was the first time the two had directly spoken to each other since Lady Cosgrave's arrival, and a flash of pain crossed Honoria's face at Amy's words. Then her expression hardened.

"You think so?" she asked coldly. "Well, perhaps you

should take care with your own words, Mrs. Harwood. I believe you've already been informed that the business of the Boudiccate is above *you,* nowadays."

Amy's expression didn't alter. But I flinched for her as she went still, and Jonathan sucked in a breath, his strong fingers flexing around my shoulders. I didn't struggle against that momentary discomfort; I knew only too well what he was feeling.

Lady Cosgrave's mouth puckered as Amy held her gaze in silence.

There wasn't time for any of this!

"There is *nothing and no one* in this nation above Amy Harwood, and you know it!" I snapped. "But I don't give a damn about the private business of the Boudiccate. Keep it as confidential as you like! All *I* care about right now is whatever you've learned about my husband. If you don't tell me where he is *right now*—"

"But Cassandra..." Lady Cosgrave sighed. "Aren't you the one who ought to be able to answer that question, as he *apparently* abandoned his duties to enjoy your company last night?"

I blinked at her, too baffled to even argue that last point. "He left Thornfell at dawn. He would have been back to his duties long before anyone even noticed—"

"He may have left *you*," said Lady Cosgrave, "but he didn't return to his post. No one has seen him since last night."

"What?" I stared at her, the world beginning to spin gently around me. "But that's not possible. He swore—"

"Didn't you even wonder what magical crisis had summoned Mr. Westgate away so urgently?" Lady Cosgrave's tone gentled, her shoulders sagging. "You must know he is always the first to be summoned whenever one of his officers of magic goes missing."

Missing.

The word pealed through me like a bell.

I hardly noticed Jonathan closing his arms around me from behind, or Amy taking my hands in a firm grip. I was floating high and untethered above my body, cut loose by that one impossible word. Their sudden stream of questions and exclamations couldn't reach me.

"He can't be missing," I said numbly to myself. "I would know..."

Wait. The words stuck in my mouth as memory suddenly swamped me.

My dream last night—then my panic this morning when I'd first awoken—it had all felt so overwhelming and so irrational. I'd felt *such* a crushing urge to check that he was safe! But of course, I had forced myself to ignore it.

How could I have been such a fool?

A door slammed in the distance, cutting off Jonathan's and Amy's agitated interrogation. Gasps sounded in the cluster of students by the library's entrance. Miss Rosenthal cried out near the back of the group, "Oh, Professor Luton, you're safe!"

Oh, for...!

At least the irritation knocked me back into myself. Ignoring the latest episode of Luton-induced chaos, I addressed Lady Cosgrave urgently. "Did Mr. Westgate tell you when he would be back?"

If not, I would have to find a magician of my own to transport me across the nation to my husband's temporary quarters...but of course, the path along the way would need to be carefully checked as well.

Wrexham had been strained to the limit by both magic and exhaustion. If his transportation spell had gone awry and landed him in danger while he was weakened by the trip... If it had turned against him entirely, as in those nightmarish warning stories of severed body parts that were told to young students as cautions for their own magical training... If he was lying injured in some isolated bog, alone and in pain, without anyone to help...

That final, much-too-vivid image froze the last of my whirling panic into icily focused determination.

He will not be left alone. No matter how many magicians I had to abduct to aid me in the search, my husband *would* be found—and quickly, too.

"*There* you are, Miss Harwood. Finally!" With a put-upon sigh, Gregory Luton pushed himself into place beside me, carelessly nudging Lady Cosgrave aside. Completely missing her outraged reaction, he tossed his hat through the air to land on the back of the closest wing-backed chair and ran both hands through his rumpled lion's mane of golden locks. Casually, he plucked out a single green leaf. "I thought I'd never hunt you down!" he said. "This place is an utter madhouse tonight. No one to be found in the dining hall despite the lateness of the hour; all of that food going to waste; no one out in the gardens but scowling servants—and there's a great big fence sticking up around my house, which I *think* I should have been consulted about beforehand! There wasn't so much as a doorway cut into it, so I couldn't even change my clothes before I—"

"Professor Luton!" I had been pushed beyond all womanly endurance. "*No one cares* about your attire. Right now we are attempting to address various important and urgent issues—"

"Why do you think I've been trying and *trying* to find you?" Luton shook his head at me pityingly. "Fey are notoriously bad listeners, you see, no matter how clearly anyone tries to explain the most obvious of magical points to them. I finally had to give up on getting through to her, myself, at all. But still..."

Shrugging, he dropped his gaze from mine and straightened his cravat with care. "I thought you'd wish to know: that fellow Wrackham—Wreckham?—whatever your husband's name may be"—he waved one hand dismissively —"he's been a prisoner in those woods of yours for hours, and things are getting dashed unpleasant in there. If you want any chance at seeing him again, you should probably do something about it."

13

I still remembered my mother's first lesson to me, which she'd repeated again and again in her nursery visits: *"You're a Harwood, Cassandra. Never forget that! Work hard, hold fast, never let anyone see your fear—and you will astonish the world with your accomplishments."*

In that, if in no other area of my life, I had listened to her. Over the decades, I had thrown myself at every seemingly impossible challenge with passionate determination and my head held high before all onlookers. Even after last year's spectacular, life-shattering failure, I had somehow convinced myself that I could build new dreams from the ashes of my old ones, and *this time*, if only I worked hard enough and held fast to my vision, *it would all work...*

And this was the moment to which that path had led me. At that realization, every difficult, distracting emotion drained away, leaving me finally, perfectly at peace.

I knew exactly what I had to do.

My voice, when it emerged, sounded pleasingly cool and steady. "Would you all please excuse me?" *There.* No one could object to that request, surely.

From the reactions of everyone around me, I might as well have shouted the most violent profanities.

"Cassandra?" Amy's grip on my arm tightened as her voice rose with unhidden alarm. "What are you doing?"

Lady Cosgrave's brows drew into an ominous frown. "I beg your pardon? Cassandra—"

"Did you not hear what I just said?" Luton demanded. "Your own husband—"

"Thank you," I murmured. "All of you. I heard what you said. Now I need a moment, please." As gently as I could, I tugged forward, and my relatives' hands fell reluctantly away.

"Cassandra..." Jonathan began.

"Thank you," I repeated sweetly, and started for the door.

My students were all clustered around it, wide-eyed and looking terribly worried. I smiled reassuringly as I gestured for them to clear my path.

"Miss Harwood—!"

"Miss Harwood—?"

"Miss Harwood," Miss Banks began, "can I—"

"I'd prefer to be alone now," I told them all, "but don't worry. Everything will be fine." I glided through the doorway with perfect ease, ignoring the swarm of panicked whispers that erupted behind me.

Really, I wasn't raging or bellowing impassioned threats. I couldn't imagine why everyone was reacting so dramatically.

Giving a pleasant smile to the maid I passed, I walked at a perfectly steady pace through the house to the study where I had locked up my most dangerous books of magic, the ones I'd never dare allow any impressionable student to find. These spells weren't only dangerous to their intended victims; they could easily kill the mage who wielded them if any mistakes were made along the way.

Luckily, in this case that risk was irrelevant. Casting any spell in the world would kill me anyway.

I was in the midst of unlocking the cabinet where they were kept when the door burst open behind me.

"Cassandra!" It was Jonathan, panting as if he had run all the way. He shoved one hand through his thick hair as he looked me frantically up and down. "You're still here."

"Of course I am." Sighing, I waved my free hand at him in dismissal. "Everything's *fine*. You needn't worry. I simply need to be alone, so—"

"Did you find her?" Amy skidded into the room after her husband, her silk slippers skating across the wooden floor. She caught hold of his arm for balance as our gazes crossed. "Thank goodness." Her shoulders sagged. Then her brown eyes narrowed as she looked past me to the cabinet with its multiple locks, half of them hanging open. "What exactly are you planning, Cassandra?"

I loved my sister-in-law, so I forced myself not to roll my eyes at the inanity of her question. "I'm going to get my husband back, of course. But as I was just telling Jonathan, I don't require any assistance, so—"

"Of course you do," Amy snapped. "There isn't a single qualified magician in this house. How do you expect to fight a wild fey without magic?"

"I *don't*," I said patiently, "but I won't have to...because you're wrong." Turning my back to the cabinet, I crossed my arms and met her gaze head-on. "There *is* a qualified magician here who knows exactly what to do."

"No," Amy breathed. For once, all of her careful, articulate arguments seemed to have deserted her. "No, no, *no*!"

"Don't be an idiot, Cassandra!" My older brother had

paled at my words, but it only made his eyes look more vividly blue as he glared at me. "You know what every single physician said. If you cast any spell, no matter how minor—"

"If I don't," I said flatly, "then *Wrexham* will die." I'd already witnessed it in my dream, hadn't I? I knew exactly how it would happen. Those vicious thorns stabbing into him again and again as the twisting green vines pinned him into place...

How had I not realized that last night's altered dream had been a warning?

Never mind. There was no time to waste on self-recriminations. I turned back to the cabinet and opened the next lock with a vengeful twist of the key. "Just keep my students safe—and *do not* allow anyone, no matter how powerful she might be, to wander off on her own for any reason! Annabel may well have summoned this creature herself, but if she didn't, then the real culprit is still hiding amongst us. She'll never dare summon it for another attack if she's surrounded by observers, though. So I'd keep everyone in one place until Wrexham or Mr. Westgate return, and then—"

"Stop!" Amy's hand closed around my arm, wrenching me around to face her furious expression. "Cassandra, *stop.* Take a moment to think about what you're doing!"

"I don't *have* a moment to waste!" The words broke out of my chest like a cry of pain, nearly shattering the careful shield I'd built for myself ever since Luton had first spoken. I *needed* that shield to do what had to be done next—but it was nearly impossible to maintain it as Amy glared at me with hurt and fear in her beloved brown eyes.

"Why do you think Wrexham's trapped in there?" I demanded, flexing my fingers restlessly by my sides. "He went in there because of me. He was trying to protect *me!*"

I could see it all so clearly. He'd sworn to leave the estate at dawn—so, as soon as I'd fallen safely asleep in his arms, he must have carefully disentangled himself and set off into the woods to investigate our fey menace for himself before the agreed-upon deadline could arrive.

All day, as I'd taught classes and managed one crisis after another, he'd been imprisoned in my woods, tangled and helpless *because of me*.

Westgate had been right about everything.

"He went in there to protect you, you say?" Jonathan's voice rose from a near-whisper to a bellow. "Then how do you think he'd feel about you running in there after him and *killing yourself*?"

"*I don't care!*" I shouted back at my brother, as the last shards of my shield collapsed entirely. "I can't sit here and do nothing while that creature tortures and murders him! Could you, if Amy were the one sitting in those woods right now?" I turned to her, my breath coming in shallow pants. "What of you? Would you sacrifice Jonathan only to keep yourself safe?"

"*No one* needs to be sacrificed tonight! And no one will be." Amy's eyes were still wide and panicked, but her voice rang like law through the room. "I mean it, Cassandra Harwood." She crossed her arms. "I am the head of this family, and I *will not* allow you to throw yourself away like this."

I gave an involuntary laugh—but it came out as a sob, jagged pain twisting through my chest. In all the years of our sisterhood, we had never once suffered life-altering conflict with each other. No matter what crises we had faced —no matter which blows the external world had flung at either of us—we had always stood unflinchingly by each other's sides.

"Amy," I said, "you should *know* me by now. When have I ever followed any rules I disagreed with?" I took a deep, unhappy breath as I slowly crossed my own arms and planted my feet more solidly on the ground. "And how exactly do you imagine you could stop me?"

Amy's eyes narrowed. I set my jaw.

"Oh, for...!" Jonathan stalked across the room to step between us with a wordless snarl. "This is an idiotic argument. Cassandra, I'll lock you up myself if it's the only way to keep you here—and Wrexham would thank me on his knees for doing it. That man loves you far too much to want to trade your life for his!"

"I can cast a spell no matter where you trap me." I kept my gaze fixed on Amy's dangerously thoughtful expression. "No matter what it takes, I *will not* spend the rest of my life knowing that I didn't do *everything I could* to save my husband."

"Argh!" My gentle, soft-spoken older brother let out a near-roar of aggravation—and the door burst open behind him.

Miss Birch looked more wild than I had ever seen her. Thin green streaks stretched like veins across the pale skin of her hands and throat, and her hazel eyes sparked with hot golden flecks. No one who saw her now could be in any doubt of the heritage she normally kept so carefully hidden.

"It's gone," she said. "That creature took it!"

"'It?'" I blinked, shifting my attention warily away from Amy's brooding expression. "If you're referring to Mrs. Renwick—"

"Not *her*." Miss Birch swept her hand through the air in contemptuous dismissal—and staggered heavily, losing her balance.

"Miss Birch!" Amy, Jonathan and I all started forward at once.

"Oh, I'm well enough." Catching herself without assistance, my housekeeper shook her head impatiently. "That creature crashed through my shields so hard, I was on my back and out of my senses for a good long while. But I'm back to work now, and if he or she imagines I'll cower away in fear like a worm—!" She glowered fiercely at all three of us.

"Of course not!" Jonathan said hastily. "No one could ever be so foolish. But mayn't I please pull out a chair for you? Just for a moment, for your comfort?"

"Who cares for comfort? I've been trying to tell you, that ring, the one from the cursed altar—"

"Altar?" Amy repeated blankly.

She and Jonathan exchanged a mystified look. He shrugged.

"You hadn't told them about it?" Miss Birch's eyebrows shot up. "I thought we were only keeping it secret from those inspectors."

I flinched as Amy and Jonathan both turned on me. "I hadn't had an opportunity yet," I muttered to all three of them.

The fog of disbelief and unspoken reproach that rose around me at that statement was thick enough to choke upon.

"I've been *busy*," I snarled. "I was summoned away from our conversation this morning, if you recall. Ever since, I've been chasing one crisis after another—"

"And last night, when it first happened?" Amy frowned. "You know perfectly well how often we're awake with Miranda. If you'd only sent over a note, we could have come—"

"Argh!" I scowled back at her. "We don't have time to argue about this. I *know* what the two of you are enduring right now. I know how desperate you've been for sleep, *and* what you've already given up for my sake! So I was hardly going to drag you from your bed last night, and I will *not* drag you into every crisis I face. I *will* solve some problems for myself rather than allowing you two to be hurt—*again* —by them!"

"And we must feel deeply grateful for that." Jonathan's tone was so dry, it scraped against my skin. "Because, *obviously,* neither of us—or your niece—could possibly be hurt *at all* by the way you're planning to launch yourself at your latest crisis. Isn't that right, Amy?"

"*No one* is going to take any more risks except for me," I gritted through my teeth. "No one else will be punished for any more of my failures. That is the entire point—"

"Oh, Cassandra, you *fool.*" Amy took two quick steps forward and grasped my shoulders, her eyes gleaming with unshed tears. "What failures? Your school and your husband have both been attacked by outsiders. You can't assume responsibility for evils that other people—"

"I'm responsible for *myself,*" I snapped, "and I should have gone after him hours ago. I should have known!" Somehow, my hands had closed around hers; I only realized it as our fingers clenched around each other. "I could have known—I would have figured it out hours ago, if I'd only stopped to think! I've been lurching from one disaster to the next, not managing any of them well enough. I didn't even have the simple wits to put the pieces together—"

"Because you've been trying to do everything yourself," Amy said firmly, "as *always.*" She gave my shoulders a gentle shake. "I swear, Cassandra, sometimes you seem to forget you even *have* a family."

"Pfft." I sniffed to pull myself together. "According to Lionel Westgate, my fatal flaw is that I'm far too much a Harwood."

"Hmmph," said Amy. "If you have any flaws, we are here to balance them—just as you do ours. That's what family is for. It's why we're *always* strongest together." She shook her head at me. "How could you possibly imagine that it wouldn't hurt us to lose you?"

"You've given up too much for me already. Your career, your closest friendship—"

"I made the decisions I believed in." Amy's tone was unbending. "I followed my principles. If you think I regret *any* of that, you haven't been paying enough attention to what I care most about. I told you: I want to change our country for the better, and this school, *right here*, is doing that. So for goodness' sake, don't shut me out of it!"

"*Or* me," added my brother, looking hangdog. "If you think I spent all those years sneaking you the key to Father's library of magic only for you to lord it over me now because I can't do any special spells myself—"

"That is *not*—! Oh, Jonathan!" I slitted my eyes up at him as I finally spotted the smirk that he'd been trying to hide. Despite the relentless ticking of the clock within my head, I couldn't help but groan. "That was a *terrible* joke to make in any circumstance."

"I could make far worse," my brother told me. "I could pretend I wouldn't mind losing my baby sister, as if it wouldn't rip out half of my heart to have you killed. *That* wouldn't be funny, would it? Or I could tell you it would be fine for Miranda to lose her only aunt." He shook his head. "Who would ever stand up for her against us, with you gone? Or tell her to ignore all the old-fashioned rules we set?"

"Who will ever give her a chance to learn magic if you give up and let this school close down now?" Amy added.

I squeezed my eyes tightly shut as every unanswerable question rose up to besiege me. I'd been trying so hard not to think of any of them.

"I can't let Wrexham die," I said. "I *cannot*."

"Then *don't*," said Jonathan. "But don't save him by killing yourself! For once, give up your precious pride and let other people help you. You don't have to do it all alone!"

I opened my eyes and found Amy looking at me from scant inches away, her brown eyes dangerously perceptive and her fingers still clasped warmly around my shoulders. "We're doing this for *us*," she said quietly, "not for your sake. We're doing what's necessary to make *ourselves* happy. And we're not the only ones who will be affected if you lose this particular battle. Every single one of those young women in the library is depending on your victory *and* your survival— not to mention all the other magical girls and women of the future."

"*And* the non-magical boys," added my brother quietly. "We all need those stifling old dichotomies to be knocked askew, for all our sakes. Men need to find our own paths in life, too."

The door opened behind him before I could answer— and this time, my entire class of students piled through it. Miss Banks led the others, her fair cheeks flushed.

"Forgive us for the interruption, Miss Harwood," she said, "but we've been listening to your discussion."

"I beg your pardon?" Stepping away from Amy, I cocked one authoritative, outraged eyebrow. "If you've been pressing your ears against the door of my private office—"

Miss Stewart cleared her throat. "We've been using a spell, actually—I found it in my uncle's library last summer.

It's quite...clever?" Her voice lilted, turning the statement into a hopeful question.

"We didn't let either of those inspectors overhear it, though," Miss Hammersley added hastily. "We left *them* listening to Mr. Luton's theories about the proper management of woodland."

"Poor Honoria," Amy murmured.

"Nonetheless!" I heaved a sigh. "You know perfectly well—"

"What we *know* is that Mr. Harwood is right," said Miss Banks. "It is time to let other people help you."

Earlier in the day, I'd glimpsed confusion and even suspicion on some of my new students' faces, as they'd wrestled over whether to listen to me or to the visiting members of the Boudiccate. Nothing that I'd said to them earlier had been enough to wipe away that uncertainty entirely.

Apparently, what my students had actually needed was a moment to listen to *each other*, without any older figures trying to tell them what to think.

Now the young women who stood behind Miss Banks— eight girls of different heights, ages, skin colors, and backgrounds—all nodded in grim agreement as she finished, looking me directly in the eyes: "You do have other practicing magicians in this house, and *all* of us need this school to survive. So—whether you care for it or not, Miss Harwood—we are coming to face that creature in the woods with you."

❧ 14 ❧

I had never in my life felt so torn between glowing pride and abject horror.

It took a long moment before I could summon words through my suddenly tight throat. "I appreciate your offer," I said, looking from one strong, determined young face to another, "far more than I could ever possibly express. But you must know that I cannot accept it. I am your *teacher*. I made a commitment to protect you all."

"It's not protecting us," said Miss Hammersley fiercely, "to make us sit here twiddling our thumbs whilst you get killed and our school closes forever!" Her accent thickened as she spoke, her freckled skin flushed scarlet, and she rubbed nervously at the frayed ends of her cuffs, but her classmates all nodded immediate agreement.

"Besides," said Miss Stewart, "we're hardly children. I'm one-and-twenty, and Julianna"—she nodded warmly to Miss Banks—"is nearly three-and-twenty. We've no need to be protected from our own decisions."

"We want to help ourselves," Miss Banks added, echoing

Amy. "We *need* this school. I know it was your idea in the beginning, Miss Harwood, but it's not only yours anymore. It's our future."

"I understand," I murmured. There was *so much* shining magical potential in this room. The idea of all of these young women being sent back to their families, their dreams snatched away and their education lost... "But the truth is, you're still young and untrained, and this is too dangerous for any of you." As their faces hardened before me, visibly refusing to accept the truth of my words, I looked to Amy for support. "*You* tell them!" My sister-in-law could find the right words to persuade anybody.

But she slowly shook her head. "How young and untrained were you, Cassandra, when you first started taking perilous risks for the sake of your magical future?"

"Oh, for—that is *not* the point!" I stared at her in outraged disbelief. "I *had* to take those risks. I had no choice! No one would *ever* have agreed to teach me magic if I hadn't."

"And no one is ever going to teach these girls, either," said Amy, "if you don't allow them to follow *your* example and take a risk or two to win their futures."

"Have you forgotten exactly how *my example* ended?" I let out a half-laugh, half-sob as I stepped back another inch from everyone else in the room, wrapping my arms around my chest. "When I took my last risk, I *lost my magic*. Do you think I would ever, for *any* reason, put a student of mine in that kind of danger?"

"But Miss Harwood..." Miss Banks's pale eyebrows furrowed in concentration. "You lost your magic because you took those risks *alone*. You had to, to prove women could be magicians, because you were the only one available. But look at us now!" She swept out an arm to indicate her assembled classmates. "*We're* not alone, any of us...because of you."

It was such a simple statement. But for a moment, I couldn't breathe as I absorbed it.

"That's the trouble with being the first, isn't it?" Amy's tone was gentle but unrelenting. "You may have had our family's support, but none of us could help when it came to magic. So I think you forgot, over the years, that even a truly remarkable, groundbreaking woman *can* let others work by her side."

"And how many more people will be hurt if I let them?" Bitterness coated my throat; I swallowed hard, fighting to keep my voice calm. "You say you don't regret giving up your own career for Thornfell—but I found out last night that Wrexham lost *his* dream, too, because of mine...and that was *before* he went into those damnable woods this morning."

I'd expected sympathy or horror in response to my awful revelation. Instead, Amy let out a bright peal of laughter. "I don't believe that for an instant! Have you ever actually *asked* Wrexham what his greatest dream is?"

My eyebrows snapped together. How ignorant did she imagine I was about my husband? "He could have been the chief magical officer for the Boudiccate if it weren't for this school. Mr. Westgate told me so last night!"

"And I know that *you* would have loved that post for yourself. But do you genuinely believe that that was ever *Wrexham's* greatest dream?" Amy shook her head at me pityingly. "Oh, Cassandra. How can you be so very clever when it comes to understanding magic...and so very, very *not* when it comes to understanding other people?"

I blinked rapidly, caught off-balance. "What—?"

"Ahem." Miss Birch cleared her throat. "If you ladies don't mind putting off the rest of your conversation..." She tilted her head at the window, where the sky was rapidly darkening. The green streaks had faded from her skin since she'd first charged into the room, but her eyes glinted with gold flecks as she finished drily, "I believe you're still in a hurry?"

"Yes." I let out my breath in a whoosh. "Of course you're right."

There was no more time for arguments—and even I could tell when I had lost a battle for good.

I might not always understand other people, but right now, I didn't have to. I had Amy and Jonathan to manage that. With the two of them by my side, I could safely focus on the magical issues whilst my students managed the active spell-casting...and Miss Birch's first words, when she'd entered the room, had been nagging at the back of my mind ever since.

"Tell me again," I told her. "The ring's gone missing? When exactly did that happen?"

"When that creature broke through all of my barriers." Her lips pursed as if she'd bitten into something sour. "I'd been looking it over just beforehand, trying to siphon any old kinships from it without luck. I'd swear it hasn't been worn on any human finger in the past month, at least. But when I woke up, it was gone."

"So someone took it." But why had it been sacrificed in the first place, if its owner never even wore it? For a sacrifice to successfully seal a fey bargain, it had to carry real emotional value. "Was the door left open?"

"Didn't need to be." She grimaced. "The magic of the completed bargain claimed it."

"*Completed*?" I blinked, twice. "That can't be right. Abducting Mrs. Renwick couldn't be enough to complete a full bargain of mischief against Thornfell. We haven't even been forced to close down yet, or—"

"What bargain?" Jonathan demanded. "You still haven't told us anything!"

I gave an impatient shrug, directing my rapid explanation at the entire company. "Someone set out an altar in the library last night. It had all the usual sorts of illicit offerings to summon fey help, including blood to seal a very nasty bargain—and one silver ring, too, but none of us recognized it."

"Yet you *still* didn't summon me?" Amy sighed. "Never mind. Just tell me now: what did it look like?"

"Plain. Silver. Thin. Unremarkable." I looked to Miss Birch. "Anything else?"

"I found a bit of hidden writing inside it this afternoon," she told me. "It took a deal of poking and experimenting to bring it up, and I'd only just managed that before the creature arrived...but it looked like curly gibberish to me. I would have shown it to you if we still had it, but—"

"Hmm." I frowned harder. Hidden writing masked in silver? "That sounds like—"

"Oh, *no*." Amy's face twisted with what looked like pain. Pressing her lips tightly together, she pulled her well-used silver pencil and commonplace book from a hidden pocket in her gown and started scribbling intently. A moment later, she held up the open book, angling it carefully so that only my housekeeper and I could see it. "Did it look anything like this, Miss Birch?"

Curving, elegant lines scrolled across the creamy paper, written in a language never seen by most people this far south of the elven kingdom...and my housekeeper's eyes widened. "That it did! What is it, then?"

Hurrying footsteps sounded through the open doorway.

"Out of my way!" Lady Cosgrave's voice rang out with the full force of her authority, sending my clustered students scattering before her.

I smiled grimly as the pieces all finally linked together. "Indeed," I said, "let us invite the former *ambassadress to the elven kingdom* to join us, shall we? I believe we may have found something that belonged to her."

☙❧

WITH ANNABEL GONE, LADY COSGRAVE HAD BEEN MY ONLY real suspect left. Even I knew I'd been contorting logic to an unreasonable extent, earlier, when I'd reasoned out all the ways that Annabel could still somehow have been our fey's summoner.

But sick betrayal still coiled in my stomach as Lady Cosgrave stepped into the room and I met her familiar, commanding gaze.

Honoria Cosgrave had been a firm feature of my life ever since I'd been a child. She'd been a warm, familiar presence for years before this visit—a true friend of the family, if not of my own, and a woman I'd trusted to *never* break the laws of our land in such a vicious fashion.

She might hate the very concept of my school. She might be furious at me. But how could she have developed such a festering hatred that she'd risk everything to end us?

None of my students had been close enough to see those elven lines written in Amy's commonplace book, but I heard a hiss of indrawn breath from Miss Banks. That sound made me glance at her, catching her wince as she glanced from

Lady Cosgrave to her own fiancée. Miss Fennell's amber eyes were wide and wary. While her strong-boned face remained set in neutral lines, her intelligent gaze darted around the room, clearly searching for clues.

Poor Miss Fennell. Even through my blazing rage, I felt a sliver of pity as I saw how rigidly she held herself. She'd been balancing between two worlds for months, keeping everything she felt so carefully closed off from view that even her closest family and mentor couldn't glimpse it. All of her secrets were finally coming to roost now, though—because all of her disagreements with her aunt had been kept private. To the outside world, she was known only as Lady Cosgrave's brightest protégée. How could she not be caught up in the political fall-out once her aunt's treachery was revealed?

Miss Stewart tucked a protective hand around Miss Banks's arm and tugged her backward, setting clear battle lines as the two Boudiccate inspectors swept past. Miss Banks's lips turned down unhappily...but she followed her new friend's guidance.

"Don't look away from me, Cassandra Harwood," Lady Cosgrave snapped. "You know perfectly well that it's explicitly forbidden to gather your students together without us when your school is under official inspection. Even more so when one of our own members has been kidnapped! If you're trying to—"

"Honoria," said Amy gently, "where has your necklace gone?"

Lady Cosgrave sucked in a quick breath, one hand flying to her throat...where her elaborate elven necklace from earlier still lay. That contradiction was enough to make me frown—but she swallowed visibly as she met Amy's gaze.

"Every day since we first met," Amy said, "you've worn a

thin silver chain hidden beneath any other necklace...a chain with a plain silver ring that hung from it. Just once, that chain broke in front of me as you were propping up a fire. I picked up the ring from the hot stones near the fireplace where it had fallen."

Aha.

Lady Cosgrave swallowed before drawing herself back up to her full height with a visible effort. "I don't know—"

"Well, of course you don't know where it is anymore." I picked up the lead from my sister-in-law, who gave me a subtle nod of agreement. "It was claimed by your co-conspirator tonight, when your illegal fey bargain was fulfilled." I shook my head, grim satisfaction battling with rising fury. "After all of your self-righteous lectures about the good of the nation and how determined *you* were to protect young women, you set a powerful, malevolent fey to attack a whole school full of them!"

"I did *not*!" High color flushed Honoria Cosgrave's cheeks beneath her silk turban. "Even if you had a single shred of evidence that I had *ever* been involved in any private fey bargaining—"

"Oh, Honoria." Amy sighed, and Jonathan shifted to stand behind her, a silent wall of support. "Don't make this even more painful."

"I would *never* put innocent young women at risk," Lady Cosgrave finished. "Never!"

I let out an involuntary crack of laughter. "I beg your pardon? You *blood-bargained with a fey* to attack our school—"

"I did no such thing." She bit out the words. "No matter how strongly I disapprove of your reckless, irresponsible choices—"

"*My* irresponsible choices?"

"I would never condone such an indiscriminate attack." At my look of open disbelief, she waved imperiously at my staring students and at her own younger cousin, who had paled and stepped backward, looking stricken. "Well? Do you see any injured or abducted young women among *their* numbers?"

"That was pure good fortune! If that creature had chosen any other bedroom to attack first..." I stumbled to a halt, my eyes widening. *Of course!*

True, those vines had tried to search Luton's house for their target this morning when they'd been repelled by Thornfell's own defenses. But when the fey who controlled them had been re-summoned within the walls of Thornfell itself, they had shot directly up to Annabel Renwick's room...

And the bargain had been completed.

"It was never about Thornfell at all," I said blankly. "You weren't even thinking about me *or* my school...except as collateral damage to your own personal schemes."

Lady Cosgrave's nostrils flared. "I told you, no one else was going to be hurt—"

"But *my school* would have been forced to close down due to the scandal if we hadn't discovered the true culprit. *Your* clever little bargain would have been taken as evidence that *I* wasn't providing a safe home for my students!"

I shook my head slowly as I looked at the master politician before me. "In other words...you would have accomplished two goals at once. You would have freed yourself from an inconvenient blackmailer *and* ended the debate over women and magic...by participating in a forbidden magical rite that I would *never* engage in myself. You hypocrite, Honoria Cosgrave! You weren't trying to protect the innocent at all. All *you* wanted was to cover up your own personal indiscretions!"

"I—"

"Wait!" Amy stepped between us, her voice firm—and compassion shining in her eyes. "Cassandra, wait." She looked past me to her former friend, who stood alone in the room. Everyone else had drawn their skirts away...even her cousin.

Amy, though, put one gentle hand on Lady Cosgrave's stiff shoulder. "I remember," she said, "those walks we used to take together around the grounds of this estate, Honoria, and how we sometimes discussed the local fey traditions. Neither of us has ever known or cared much about magic—but *everyone* knows that a fey bargain must be sealed with a true sacrifice.

"And..." She gave a rueful smile. "I know you, Honoria Cosgrave—even if you no longer wish to know me. So I *know* you would never wear such a plain piece of jewelry hidden around your neck for all these years if it didn't hold a vital piece of your heart. You care more about the welfare of the women of this nation than any other politician I know. So why don't you give in and simply tell us all now: who *were* you protecting with that fey bargain, to make such a terrible act worthwhile?"

Lady Cosgrave stayed silent for a long, frozen moment.

Then she said, very quietly, "It wasn't that I didn't wish to know you, Amy. I had no choice in the matter."

Glowering, I opened my mouth for a hot retort—but my sister-in-law silenced me with a look.

"I do know," she said to her former friend. "Annabel forced it, didn't she?"

Lady Cosgrave moistened her lips with a quick flick of her tongue. "It is...painful to give up a friendship," she murmured. "But some threats...some dangers are even worse. And some are even more vulnerable. Some women. In nations where men control everything."

Elven writing.

Our former ambassadress.

"An elf?" I asked tentatively. "Is she a friend of yours? Or...?"

Her lips tightened, and I understood.

More than a friend.

Ohhhh. I blinked rapidly as agitated whispers rose from our crowded onlookers, all of us absorbing the revelation together.

Fey-human matches like the one that had borne Miss Birch might be considered shocking by small-minded people even now, in our supposedly enlightened era. But it was genuinely unheard of for any haughty elf and a mere human to conduct a liaison...and after the wars that had scarred our nation's history, the thought even carried a faint, leftover whiff of treason.

That revelation might well have sunk her political career for good, whether or not the affair had taken place before her sensible marriage to a gentleman magician—the sacrifice that she'd told her cousin every politician must simply accept.

Honoria, though, would never be the one to suffer most if the truth ever came out. In the hopelessly masculine elven kingdom, as she had reminded me this morning, ladies were considered the legal property of their husbands or male relatives. The punishments for any elven lady who flouted their archaic rules of 'purity' were known to be astonishingly brutal.

Now I knew why Honoria had railed so passionately about the horrors of their system—and why they had felt so fresh in her mind. What threats had Annabel been whispering in her ears for all these months?

"Annabel was going to tell the elves, too, wasn't she?" I breathed. "If you didn't do everything she told you—"

"Or for simple amusement," Lady Cosgrave said bitterly, "if she ever tired of playing with me. She said as much, the last time I tried to argue against one of her unreasonable demands. It *might* never have happened, if she'd decided it was more amusing to keep me in suspense forever...but." She sighed, and slid a sidelong glance at her young cousin. "There were always fresh scandals brewing, she said, that could be used to keep any future members of the Boudiccate in line."

The last of the color drained from Miss Fennell's face. Miss Banks made a quick, abortive movement toward her and then stilled.

"Honoria," Miss Fennell began, her voice thick with emotion.

"Enough." Lady Cosgrave gave a quick, warning shake of her head. "I have made my own decisions, now and always. And I will allow *no one* to hurt anyone in my care."

Well. I straightened my shoulders, adjusting to the new situation. "Neither will I," I told her firmly. "This school is not a pawn to be sacrificed. Nor is my husband."

"Oh, for—!" She closed her eyes and sucked in what looked like a sustaining breath. "I told you, I *never* directed that creature to—"

"You may not have *asked* it to attack anyone but Annabel Renwick," I said, "but you summoned it into this house, unleashing it from the old agreement that kept it safely off our grounds. And he went into those woods hunting it because of you." I took a step closer as her eyes reluctantly reopened. "So, *right now*, Honoria Cosgrave, I want you to tell us everything you know about the fey holding Wrexham...

"And then we are going to walk into those woods with my students to save my husband *and* our school and complete a *very* different bargain."

❧ 15 ❧

We left Thornfell fifteen minutes later with a grumbling Gregory Luton in tow. We'd swept him up from the meal he'd been busily devouring alone in the dining hall, and he still held a chicken leg impaled by his supper-knife as he trailed after us into the dimly-lit foyer, complaining all the way.

"I *told* you, I spent hours trying to talk sense into that blasted fey already. If you imagine that *I* could persuade her—"

"I wouldn't even ask you to try." I flung open the great front doors. Outside, the sky spread dark blue above the trees, fading gently into black. The lanterns hanging from our hands shone in the evening air like golden, clustered stars. "Trust me, Mr. Luton, I haven't collected you for your diplomatic skills. As everyone in Angland knows, you haven't any."

"Hmmph." He took a large bite, glowering, while our surrounding students variously watched us with wide-eyed interest or pretended not to be listening with all their might. "Why bother hauling me along at all, then?"

"I'm not accomplished at diplomacy, either," I admitted —both to him and to our listeners. There was no use in pretending anymore that I was always flawlessly in control, no matter how hard I'd fought to present that deceptive façade earlier. By now, my students had all witnessed my deepest and rawest vulnerabilities...and yet, miraculously, they were all still here, gathered around me, and even more committed to our school now that they weren't simply following my instructions without question.

"We each have our own particular strengths. And"—I slid a rueful glance at my sister-in-law, who gave me an equally rueful smile from her position at Lady Cosgrave's side—"I've been reliably informed that *no one* can succeed every time on their own. Together, we may yet work wonders."

Now that I was finally leading the way to Wrexham, every factor but efficiency had dropped away. It was a drum-beat throbbing through my skin, the compulsion to reach him before anything worse could happen.

"Just tell me," I told Luton as I led our group into the cool darkness, "exactly what you saw today."

I knew from Lady Cosgrave that the fey was female. I knew from my dreams that she hated my family.

What a gift it must have seemed to her, for a Harwood's husband to walk into her woods just when Honoria's bargain had unleashed her full malice.

"As I *tried* to tell you earlier," he said wearily, "I was up late working on my lesson plans when I saw your husband walk into the woods. I thought perhaps no one had mentioned the danger to him—or he'd forgotten it—so when he still hadn't come out an hour later, I thought I'd better take a look."

"Despite the danger?" Amy asked.

"And without mentioning it to anyone else first?" Jonathan added.

Luton snorted. "I hardly feared any fey for my own sake. *I* can protect myself perfectly well!"

Miss Stewart let out a dreamy sigh behind me, while our other students rustled with interest and the shell-lined drive crunched beneath our feet.

Shielded by the growing darkness, I rolled my eyes and stepped off the drive onto the cool grass. "*Regardless*," I said.

The woods bulked thickly ahead of our lantern-cast light, deep and shadowy and secret. Somewhere inside it, that fey and her thorns were lurking, waiting for me in the dark.

She had to know I'd be coming for him. Harwoods never, *ever* abandoned their family. That was the unyielding truth that had kept us strong for centuries. It had built this estate and my family's political and magical legacies, too.

If she was laying a trap for me now, I would step into it with my eyes wide open. Miss Birch had remained behind to protect Thornfell; it would be waiting, strong and safe, for my students to return to even if I fell in the woods tonight.

"There's not much more to say." Luton shrugged. "She's a typical fey. No interest in any intellectual debates or logic. Wouldn't let him go or even engage in a simple magical duel to sort it out like gentlemen."

He'd suggested a magical duel to a fey? As my eyebrows rose, I reluctantly accepted the unpalatable truth: I would *never* be able to sack Gregory Luton, after all. No one who had risked his life so recklessly to save my husband could ever be allowed to lose his safe haven at my school.

It was an utterly disheartening realization, but I swallowed it down as I raised my lantern before me and ducked my head below the first overhanging branches to step inside the deeper darkness of the bluebell woods...and into fey territory.

A cool breeze rustled through the leaves above me, carrying a faint, eerie echo of distant horns. The sound shivered across my skin, sending goosebumps prickling across my body.

Whenever the bluebells opened, the veil between worlds in these woods became thinner than the finest gauze, allowing the fey to move seamlessly between them. Who knew where those horns were truly sounding? Or what wild hunt might be taking place in these very woods tonight?

No human could ever be safe in these woods tonight. But no one turned back. We all clumped together to form a tightly huddled mass, and I turned to Mr. Luton.

"We'll follow your directions through the woods to find her."

"Miss Harwood?" Miss Hammersley's voice shivered behind me. "I don't think we'll need to."

She held up her lantern, followed by all of the others...and their gathered glow revealed a long, thick green vine, studded with glistening thorns, lying curled and waiting on the grass before us, twitching with impatience like a serpent preparing to strike.

I sucked in a breath. Before I could speak, it unspooled its curves, rapidly shook itself out, and then turned and flowed sinuously away into the woods...just slowly enough for us to follow.

"So." My voice shook, but I took a purposeful step forward. "I believe we have our directions."

"This is absurd," Lady Cosgrave muttered as we all shuffled forward together. Her voice was low, but in the throbbing darkness of the woods, it carried easily to my ears. "Amy, *you* at least must see sense: there is no *purpose* in us all sacrificing ourselves together. This is a matter for magicians, not politicians—"

"And yet you, Honoria, are the one who invited that creature—*twice*—into Cassandra's home, creating this danger in the first place." Amy's voice was perfectly cool and utterly inflexible, and despite everything, my lips curved with pride as I picked my way forward through the darkness, listening.

She had taken Lady Cosgrave's arm as we'd first set out, in what might have seemed a friendly gesture—but when Jonathan had closed in on Lady Cosgrave's other side, I'd understood that they were working together, as always, to box her in at the center of our group.

"Perhaps," Amy continued sweetly now, "if you'd wished to stay safely out of fey affairs, you might have *seen sense* yourself before choosing to mortally imperil my family and betray all our years of friendship."

That winding, teasing tail of the fey's vine slithered ahead, just within the farthest circle of our lanterns' light. The scent of wild garlic blossomed and clouded in the air around us, its leaves hidden in the darkness but crushed by our heavy feet. We'd left the smoother, tamer, established path behind. Now, sticks and tree roots crunched with every step as we made our way up an angled slope, between dangling branches that poked and stabbed at my eyes, while curving leaves stroked and clung to my hair.

Lady Cosgrave sucked in a breath behind me. "I *told* you why I had to make those decisions! I thought you understood—"

"Oh, I do," murmured Amy, "and I could easily forgive you for dropping my acquaintance. But the moment you chose *my sister-in-law's home* as the setting for a fey assassination attempt, placing my family in mortal danger—"

"That was *never* my intention or—"

"Shhh!" I hissed, coming to a halt.

The thorny tail of our guiding vine had just disappeared, whipping with a sudden burst of speed up a tree, through its leaf-heavy branches, and out of sight. I rose to my tiptoes, raising my lantern high and casting its glow as far as it would spread. Our group came to a ragged standstill behind me. We huddled together, darkness pressing in around our lanterns.

Quick, unsteady breaths sounded behind me, unreasonably loud to my ears. My heartbeat thudded in my throat. Something snuffled low to the ground nearby, grass rustling by my feet. I clenched my fingers tightly around my lantern to keep myself still. As I took a deep, sustaining breath, a tawny owl cried mournfully through the trees like a warning—and behind me, one of my students let out a muffled whimper.

That did it. Fury subsumed my own fear, and I stepped forward, jerking free of the protection of our group.

"Well?" I called out to the creature who hid in the darkness, as Amy and Jonathan stepped up behind me. "What are you waiting upon? I'm here, where you wanted me. You needn't settle for lurking about my dreams anymore."

A woman's low laughter sounded, uncomfortably close but impossible to locate. It had a jagged, broken edge, and it seemed to come from before me and from my left, both at once. "Ah, you truly are a Harwood, aren't you? I know that imperious tone so well." Grass rustled suddenly around my feet in a rapid, slithering circle that sent an icy chill rushing through my veins.

It was the sound of her vines, looping around me like a noose. But she wasn't drawing that noose closed—at least, not yet. She said, her tone wondering, "You never believe in the truth of your own danger, do you? You Harwoods walk into these woods and into my arms as if nothing could ever harm any of you."

At that, I choked on a bitter half-laugh of my own. "You may have invaded my dreams, but you don't know much about me if you actually believe that."

When I'd been younger, her words might well have described me. Last year, though, all of my fiercely maintained certainty in my own abilities had been shattered beyond repair. I'd spent months putting myself back together with the help of the wise, strong people who loved me—but every mistake that I'd made in these past few days had stemmed directly from my own raw pain, and fear of failing so catastrophically once again.

"It's not that I don't believe in my own danger," I told her steadily. "It simply doesn't matter as much as what I'm fighting for tonight." *My love. Our home. My school. Our future.*

I wanted to spit out threats every bit as vicious as the dreams that she had sent me. But with Amy and Jonathan standing in silent support at my back, I drew on their combined strength to summon long-ago lessons from my mother, who'd tried so hard to groom me for future political alliances. "My family has lived in harmony with the creatures of these woods for centuries. That long peace doesn't have to be broken now."

"*I* am not the one who broke that peace," she snapped, and the vines tugged closer around my feet. "It was betrayed long before today. I've only been waiting for the chance to take my payment!"

Payment? "Did someone agree to a bargain with you, then leave it unfulfilled?" I asked. "One of *my* ancestors?"

Which of them could have ever been so reckless? And how in the world had they survived it?

If any of them *had* outwitted a fey and escaped a sealed bargain, it should have been passed down as a powerful family story. Given the bigoted views that had reigned unquestioned in previous centuries, it would have been considered a proud achievement rather than a guilty secret. But when I half-turned my head to catch my historian brother's gaze, he shook his own head in a quick negative, his brows knotted.

Amy said, her tone gentle, "As head of the family, I'd like to extend our sincere apologies if any of our members have mistreated you. I'm certain we can come to a new agreement that—"

"Oh, Mrs. Harwood." Grass rustled around my feet as that unearthly voice shivered with anticipation. "Did you think I'd brought any of you here to *talk*?"

With a sudden lunge, the sharp-thorned noose yanked tightly shut around my ankles. My feet skidded out before me on the grass.

I flung my arms to my sides in absolute trust as I fell. "*Now*!" I bellowed.

Amy and Jonathan seized one arm apiece, holding me back with all of their strength as the vine tried to drag me forward. Sharp thorns pierced through my stockings into my skin, but I wasn't listening to my own moan of pain. Behind me, four young women had started shouting out a spell any Great Library graduate would recognize, while another five recited the spell we'd written together this afternoon....

And dazzling light erupted through the nighttime woods a moment later as golden bells pealed deafeningly all around us like the sound of my overflowing pride.

Crying out in surprise, the woman exposed before us stumbled back half a step into the lush spread of purple bluebells that covered the ground. As she threw her hands to her pointed ears, the noose loosened infinitesimally around my ankles.

I could never have mistaken her for a human. Her loose brown hair was streaked with green, leaves grew from its tangled strands, and her arms were as long and thin as a sapling's branches. Her tattered green and gold gown, alone, was surprisingly familiar in style—but only from portraits painted a century ago.

Still, none of her odd and startling beauty could hold my attention after I caught sight of the tree just behind her, where a thick mass of green covered a long, lanky shape...that was unmistakably human.

"*Wrexham!*" I yanked my arm free from Amy's grip and seized the supper-knife from Luton's hands. As little as magicians might like to think it, magic *wasn't* the only weapon against magic, after all.

The half-eaten chicken leg from Luton's dinner sailed away, burying itself under bluebells, as I slashed myself free from the wicked, stabbing noose. I clenched the knife handle in my fist and leaped forward, ignoring the slide of fresh blood down my feet as I aimed for that tree and the long, familiar shape beneath the vines...which wasn't moving, even now.

Why wasn't it moving?

Closer, closer—

Long, strong fingers grabbed my arm and thrust me off-balance, jagged fingernails digging into my skin like claws. "You can't have him!" Orange-flecked green eyes glared at me. "Your family stole my love. Now I have yours, and I'll kill him in front of you. Do you have *any idea* how long I've waited for this revenge?"

I glared back at her. "My family *never* harmed or abducted any fey from these woods! *We* followed the rules and—"

"You *lied*," she spat, pulling me closer. Her breath tasted of moss and blood. "*He* lied every time he saw me! I should never have let him walk in my woods. He swore that he loved me, but your family wrapped around him like a curse! He spun me dreams of living together in Thornfell in secret, under their noses, and he tricked me into believing him. He swore he would be true forever, but then he *left me* without a single word! I meant nothing to him. Nothing did, in the end, except your blasted human rules and your Harwood pride. He—"

"*He*?" Through the heat of confusion and rage, sudden clarity pierced. I turned in her grip to meet my brother's shocked gaze as my students gathered around him and the others like an army. "Wait a minute," I said.

This mysterious *he* had walked in these woods.

He hadn't dared introduce her to our family.

"Can you be talking about *Romulus Harwood*?" I asked in disbelief.

My enigmatic ancestor had baffled the world with his insistence on living here and his refusal to marry any of the women his sisters suggested to him. He'd sighed in his journal over his mysterious love—whom he could never reveal to his sisters. Finally, I understood why.

"Did he boast about it?" Her face twisted with pain. "When he left me forever without a farewell, did he laugh about how he'd managed to break an immortal fey's heart?"

"He didn't laugh." Jonathan stepped forward, his voice low and his expression awed. "And he didn't leave. Madam

—forgive me, I don't know your name. He only called you *his beloved* in his journal. But didn't you know? He died. He was only eight and thirty, but the influenza took him within days. Physicians were summoned, and magicians, too, but none of the magic in our family could save him."

The claw-like nails around my arm dug in with such a spasm of force, I gasped out loud and blood seeped from my skin. "You're lying to me again!" she snarled. "Humans are *always* deceitful. You think you can trick me with your words, just as he did—"

"We have *evidence*," I gasped, breathing shallowly through the pain. "We can prove it."

Thank goodness my family never discarded old books...and thank Boudicca I'd brought along our family historian after all.

"Just wait," I told the woman who could have been family, "and we'll show you."

❧ 16 ❧

I n the eerie stillness of the splashed-bright night woods, it seemed that Jonathan might never return.

My students held the blazing light spell steady, working together with linked arms. My gaze darted from one determined young face to another, watching for any signs of tiring. My captor's clawed grip on my arm tightened with every agonizing minute that passed, until the deep pain numbed into a steady, constant pulse as faraway and insignificant as my own heartbeat.

Jonathan would be safe on this trip. I told myself that, again and again as we waited. Mr. Luton had gone back to the house with him to serve as a magical guard along the way—and as far as I knew, no *other* fey in these woods held a special grudge against our family.

There still hadn't been a single rustle of movement from the tree where Wrexham was bound.

I tried not to look out of the corner of my eye.

I looked again and again. I couldn't help myself.

If he was—

No. She'd planned to kill him before my eyes, which meant he was still alive now. I was certain of it.

...Almost certain.

"Annabel Renwick," I said at last, my voice hoarse with pain. "The one you took. Where is she?"

There was no body to be seen apart from the one tied to the tree—and *that* was too tall to be anyone but Wrexham, even beneath all those layers of obscuring vines.

My captor shrugged irritably, her gaze still fixed in the direction that Jonathan had gone. "I did as I was bid, to fulfill my bargain. I sent *that* one through the bluebells. She won't find her way back to your world again."

Ohhh. I took a deep, steadying breath as those bluebells bobbed in the night air before me, wild and fey and eerily beautiful, much like the woman who held me in her clawed grip.

Annabel would no longer be the most powerful tormentor in her new home...and when I thought of exactly what she'd threatened for Lady Cosgrave's own beloved, I couldn't find any regret for her punishment. But I couldn't restrain a reluctant shiver of empathy, either.

I would never willingly walk by bluebells again.

After an endless amount of time, Amy took a deep breath of her own and shook out her shoulders, turning away from the darkness where her husband had disappeared. "Well, ladies," she said briskly, "there's no point wasting this time, is there?"

My captor let out a low growl. "If you think you can—"

"I beg your pardon," said Amy gently, "but I was speaking to my colleagues. The rest of you may manage the magic here, but *we*"—she looked from one Boudiccate inspector to another—"are here for the more traditional womanly arts of government. I believe this is an excellent moment to resolve them. Honoria?"

Lady Cosgrave slanted one reluctant glance at my captor and grimaced. "Oh, very well," she said, straightening her shoulders and smoothing down her dress unnecessarily. "You all know what I did, and why I did it. But if you imagine, any of you, that you'll ever get away with revealing my secrets to the world yourselves—"

"*Honoria*." Amy sighed. "You are standing in a circle of women who have *all* moved away from the expectations we were born with...including our hostess." She nodded politely to my captor. "Do you truly imagine that any of us would cast aspersions on you for whom you loved? After everything that you've heard tonight?" She gestured to the circle of women who held the spell, and then to me and to Wrexham beyond. "Do you think *we* can't all understand doing whatever it takes to keep them safe?"

A deep sigh lowered Lady Cosgrave's shoulders. "Of course not," she said quietly. Sorrow etched deep lines on her cheeks, making her look suddenly ten years older, as she looked directly at Amy for the first time since our arrival. "I do know better, Amy. *You* would never resort to blackmail."

"No," said Amy, "and I don't need to. Do I?"

Lady Cosgrave didn't answer—but her cousin, frowning, edged closer as if in preemptive defense.

"Honoria Cosgrave," said Amy, "you are the most principled politician I know. So," she finished gently, "you already know what you need to do. Don't you?"

Lady Cosgrave's fingers flexed into fists by her side. She didn't speak. Miss Fennell frowned harder.

"I know you," said Amy, "so I know exactly what you would say of any other politician who conspired toward the fey abduction and disappearance of another member of the Boudiccate, no matter *what* her justification might be. Could such a woman ever be safely left in charge of the nation, once she'd broken our oldest laws and escaped punishment?

"Moreover..." She gestured once more to my students. "Tell me, Honoria: what would she owe to the young women —*and* their partners—whom she'd recklessly endangered for that illegal purpose, no matter how justified her reasons may have been?"

She looked at my captor, and at the steady trickle of blood that dripped from my captured arm onto the blue-bells. "I think we've *all* seen tonight what truly happens when we cling to outdated social rules to the detriment of our own dreams."

Standing behind her older cousin, Miss Fennell bit her lip, looking agonized...but then she nodded in agreement, even as she took Lady Cosgrave's arm in a supportive grip.

Lady Cosgrave, who had helped to rule the nation from the time I was a little girl, closed her eyes for one long moment as we stood exposed in the magic-bright woods.

Then she opened them. "I suppose," she said quietly, "my consolation will be knowing that another woman of principle will be ready to take my place." Her lips curved into a small, wry smile. "You may never accept my friend-ship again, Amy Harwood. But you'll have my parting vote, nonetheless. So will this school."

"My vote as well," Miss Fennell said huskily. "Which makes it a majority, regardless of Westgate's choice. We cannot choose safety over hope anymore."

For her, it should have been a moment of unalloyed victory. But her face twisted with grief as she looked at her defeated cousin and mentor, and when she looked across to

Miss Banks linking arms with Miss Stewart—the two young women leaning into each other as they shared their magical strength—a flash of raw fear crossed her strong features.

With her mentor's sudden loss of power, her own path to the Boudiccate was suddenly in question. Perhaps it was natural that she would doubt everything else, too, at such a moment.

I had faith in her future, for I knew the quiet strength of her fiancée's will. But it would be up to the two of them to sort out their romance once this inspection was safely over...and even as I thought that, I heard a sound that was only too familiar: Gregory Luton's voice, raised in mid-lecture.

"...In *my* opinion, if the fey and the weather wizards worked more closely together—ah. Are we here already?"

"Finally," said my brother drily, and stepped into the circle of light, pushing a wheelbarrow laden with more than mere books.

Every volume of Romulus Harwood's journal lay piled there—and a wooden chest I'd never seen sat there, as well.

"The journals were sent to Thornfell's library," Jonathan told me, "but this chest was stored in Harwood House's attic, full of everything else that Romulus left behind. We've been storing it all these decades as a family record...but it seems to me that someone else deserves it more.

"Madam." He gave my captor a deep, respectful bow. "I believe that all of these belong to you."

Slowly, painfully, the fey woman's fingers unclenched from my arm. As fresh air stung the open wounds, I bit down hard on my tongue...and forced myself to wait.

"Show me," she said, her voice rough. In the under-growth around us, green vines slithered and snapped in a restless, undulating motion.

Jonathan scooped up the journal he'd laid at the very top of the pile, and flipped open to a page he'd marked.

"*Met with my beloved, spinning dreams together. I brought her the ivy I'd cultivated in a potte all winter, and—*"

A sob ripped out of her throat as she lunged forward, snatching for the book with her hands as her vines lunged from the grass and bluebells to wrap themselves around the wheelbarrow full of memories. Thorns poked out from every angle like barbed warnings to anyone who'd dare try to steal them from her.

Her long fingernails were red with my blood. Her green and orange eyes were inhuman.

But the tears that glimmered in them, as she turned over the next page in the journal with careful, spindly fingers, were as familiar to me as my own soul.

"It's him," she said softly. "You brought him to me. You brought him back."

"He never stopped loving you," Jonathan replied just as quietly. "You'll see that in his journals. Harwoods never abandon their partners."

The fey woman didn't answer for a long moment. Finally, she looked up from the faded pages to meet his gaze. "You have his eyes," she told him. "They were always kind eyes. They were gentle—and they were the first, of any kind, to truly see me."

Taking a step backward, she pressed the journal to her chest, her sharp-thorned vines dragging the wheelbarrow along with her into the bluebells. "You gave me these," she said. "I'll give you something in return. You'll never be in danger from me or any other fey in these woods again unless you try to steal these back from me."

Amy stepped up beside her husband, tucking her hand into the curve of his arm. "We apologize," she said, "for the hurt that you endured. But we are happy to give you every-thing we have of his now—and we hope that we may *all* move forward." Pointedly, she glanced past the other woman at me. "If you would?"

"We gave you yours," I said hoarsely. "Now I need mine."

If he was still breathing.

If I wasn't too late.

If I hadn't wasted—

No. I hadn't wasted the hours of this day. Without today's lessons, we would never be here now, lit by the glow of my students' combined magic. Amy had been right: I could never have succeeded on my own. I could have killed my enemy and myself, both at once, with one final, brutal spell —but I couldn't have *saved* anyone at all.

That took all of us, working together and yanking aside the old prejudices that had blinded all of us and kept us apart.

The fey woman looked at me with eyes that had seen deep into my dreams. "You won't see me again," she said, "but I'll see you, Cassandra Harwood. I'll watch Thornfell and keep it safe as long as you protect my woods. And I won't keep your own love from you any longer."

With a click of her long, branch-like fingers, the thickly-layered vines began to writhe around the tree behind her. The ends rushed back towards her as I rushed towards the tree...

And she was gone, vanishing into the bluebell-covered ground, by the time I reached it.

Just enough of the vines had unraveled to show familiar, silky black hair at the top. My fingers bit into my palms as I forced my hands to my sides. I didn't dare touch those writhing vines as they pulled themselves free, in case the thorns bit even harder into his flesh—but as more and more layers of vines whipped away, I sucked in a breath at what was revealed before me:

A high, light brown forehead, smooth and unmarred by wounds.

Closed eyelids that no thorn had touched.

Wrexham's beloved, angular face was stubbled and still as stone—but not hurt. Not a single thorn had scratched it.

Yet his face was so *still*, inhumanly still...ohhh. *Magically* still!

Of course.

She hadn't been the one who'd trapped him after all. Once he'd realized that he couldn't win their battle, he'd trapped *himself* in a protective shield she couldn't break...a shield that only the right person would be able to open.

He'd kept himself safe for me, as I'd asked.

Slowly, unbelieving, my lips curved into a smile that burst with joy.

It was no wonder Westgate had wanted him as the next Chief of the Boudiccate's magical officers. My husband was the *best*, cleverest, and most imaginative practicing magician in all England...and just as soon as that final vine pulled itself free—once I'd kissed him and berated him and ravished him soundly and ordered him to *never* take such a risk for me ever again!—I was going to *demand* that he teach me that brilliant new spell he'd designed that had protected him even from a malevolent fey's fury.

No one else could have thought it up except for him. Of that, I was already certain.

His eyes opened as I laid one careful hand against his cheek.

Wrexham blinked, twice, wariness replaced by startlement as he took in the whole scene with his dark, intelligent gaze. Then his mouth curved as I shook my head at him, tears of relief standing in my eyes.

"Of all the ridiculous, amazing, terrible, *wonderful* gentlemen I have *ever* known—"

"Had a good second day at work, have you, Harwood?" he inquired wryly.

Vines unknotted themselves from around his body and slithered past mine into the sea of bluebells. My students gathered around us in a semicircle of linked arms, beaming as they held the blazing spell of light, while my brother and sister-in-law stood behind them, patiently tolerating Luton's lecture on how we might have done every bit of tonight's venture differently if only we had listened to him from the beginning.

Sharp thorns brushed against my legs and sides as they swept past, but our whole community stood guard around us, and that community would only grow from now on.

"*Did I have a good day?*" I repeated incredulously.

Cupping both hands around my husband's lean cheeks, I leaned in to answer him with a kiss lit by shining magic.

T he vines had retreated from Luton's cottage by the time we finally emerged from the woods, but soft moonlight shone through the massive holes in the fencing to reveal all the wreckage left behind.

Luton looked at his cottage's broken door and groaned dramatically.

I said briskly, "Never mind. Given the circumstances, I'm sure no one will question your virtue if you choose to stay in Thornfell with the rest of us tonight. We'll find you a room well away from any ladies, with a door that locks firmly from the inside."

"Or you could sleep at Harwood House," Jonathan added, "if you're concerned about your reputation."

"No." Luton drew himself up, giving his cottage one last, wistful look before turning to Thornfell with squared shoulders. "I shan't desert my post. Besides, Mr. Wrexham will be sleeping in Thornfell tonight. With a married gentleman in residence, my reputation should be safe enough."

"*Will* I finally be sleeping there tonight?" Wrexham leaned to murmur the words into my ear, his warm breath tingling against my skin. "Or will my wife insist on sending me away yet again?"

"Don't be absurd." I narrowed my eyes up at him and tightened my possessive grip around his arm. "If you think I'm letting you out of my sight again before I *know* you're entirely recovered—"

"*I* wasn't the one who was injured," he pointed out. "I spent the day sleeping in perfect comfort as I waited for my wife to save me. Whereas..." As his gaze dropped to the wounds on my bare arm, his tone darkened. "I should think, if *either* of us was allowed to be concerned with the other's health just now—"

"We'll sort it all out later," I promised as we crossed the grass together toward the dark, familiar mass of Thornfell. Exhilaration bubbled through me as the front door opened. Miss Birch stood solidly planted in the doorway, and warm light streamed out to welcome us home. "We *will* have time tonight." For once, it could be my top priority.

First, though, there was organization to be done. It took an inordinate amount of time to re-gather my giddy, victorious students around the dining table to eat their long-awaited supper—not to mention having my own arms and ankles cleaned and bandaged *and* finding a guest bedroom that could meet Mr. Luton's own exacting standards.

I would have liked to roll my eyes and announce that he could sleep on the floor if he didn't care for any of the options...but I vividly remembered that moment, this afternoon, when I'd been so dreadfully certain of his death under my care. He'd spent that very same time arguing in the woods for Wrexham's life...so I could put up with his requirements a little longer now.

When an appropriate compromise had been painfully hammered out at last and the last of the stragglers had been collected, my students and my professor of weather wizardry all finally settled in around the long table, laughing, talking, debating, eating cold chicken and drinking Miss Birch's special hot, mulled cider, with spices that floated gorgeously through the air.

I let out a long breath of relief—and turned to where Amy waited for me, smiling, by the door.

Lady Cosgrave had chosen to take her own supper in her room that night, as had Miss Fennell, for understandable reasons. Not only was she grieving for her cousin, but her own political situation had just become infinitely more precarious. The secret of her betrothal would have to be kept a little longer, even here within the walls of Thornfell.

Jonathan, who never liked to be away from baby Miranda for long, had already gone home to confirm that all was well, while Wrexham had scooped up a plate of cold chicken and left for our room immediately after overseeing the careful bandaging of my wounds.

So Amy and I were left entirely alone as we walked, arm-in-arm, through the maze of dimly lit green-and-gold rooms that we had decorated, clocks ticking as we passed them on our way to the front door.

"Finally," I said, as I squeezed her arm close. "*Finally*! I *knew* you would be a member of the Boudiccate one day, no matter how many years it took."

"Of course you did." My sister-in-law gave me a sidelong grin, her usual serene façade breaking into an expression of dazzling mischief. "Don't Harwoods always get what we fight for...together?"

"Always." The truth of it surged up inside me. I had to swallow hard before I could speak again. "We will *always* fight together, no matter what. I promise you, Amy—I won't shut you out of any of my battles again. Not ever."

She let out a small sigh, squeezing my arm in warm return. "But I won't be here to help you after all! When I step into the Boudiccate and take on all of those duties, with so much travel around the country—"

"You'll still be a vital part of this school, no matter where you are," I told her. "You can be our official patroness, if you like, with an intimidating portrait hanging in our front hall to glower at any interlopers from now on. Can you even imagine us having a member of the *Boudiccate* as Thornfell's own patroness?"

"Well," said Amy lightly, "I suppose, if you promise not to use that truly dreadful portrait of me in red just to tease me..."

I didn't miss the tell-tale glitter of a tear in her eye as she looked quickly away from me, trying to hide it. "Yes," she finished softly, "I would like that, actually."

I leaned my head into her shoulder, slipping one arm around her soft waist. "Don't you know I'll be writing to you every day, asking for your opinion on everything I do? As always?"

"Oh, I know it," she said firmly, "because if you don't...!" Smiling ruefully, she swiped one strong brown hand across her eyes and gathered me in for a tight hug as we reached the foyer. "I'm proud of you, too," she whispered into my hair. "Now go be happy for a night. You've been working long enough for it!"

I waved her off as she disappeared down the long, familiar path to Harwood House and my first home. Then I turned.

I'd barely slept in ten days. I hadn't eaten a single bite of supper.

And there was only one place in the world that I wanted to be right now.

I gathered up my skirts and ran like a giddy girl, leaping up the public staircase two steps at a time. I skidded to a halt outside my bedroom door—

Just as Wrexham yanked it open from the inside, his black hair mussed and his face alight with happiness. "I *thought* I heard you coming," he told me—and scooped me up into his arms.

I wrapped my arms and legs around him and let the door fall shut to the sound of our mingled laughter.

As we tumbled together onto the big bed, I reached out to trace his smooth, lemon-scented cheeks wonderingly. "You've shaved!"

"Of course I did." He stroked my face, mirroring my action. "Isn't it our wedding night? At last?"

"*At last.*" Melting, I leaned in for a kiss...then caught myself and pulled back just before our lips touched. "Wait!"

A groan of pure anguish ripped from his mouth. "What? *Why?*"

"Shh." I propped myself up on one elbow to look down at him. I had important things to say before I could allow myself to be distracted. "There are *some people*," I told him carefully, "who think that I can be a tad...dictatorial from time to time when I'm making decisions for your sake. And...*some* people have pointed out that I don't always take the time to *ask* you what you actually want before I do it."

His eyes narrowed; one long, clever finger trailed distractingly down my neck, slipping gently beneath the edge of my bodice. "Harwood, if you imagine I don't want this..."

I captured that dangerous, stray finger and held it. "Wrexham," I said, "I have an idea to solve all of our problems—with your career *and* with our marriage, to bring us more time together. But I don't want to tell you what to do.

So I need to ask first: what do *you* want next? Truly? Without worrying about what I need."

My husband's dark eyebrows arched as he watched me for a long moment in silence. Then he said slowly, "Other people *have* said, from time to time, that I have a tendency to keep too many of my own thoughts private. So...you can hardly be blamed for not knowing what I'm thinking, if I've never said the words out loud."

"But I *want* to know," I said, "and it's safe to tell me. Truly."

"I know." He sighed, propping himself up on the bed beside me. "And you know I didn't form that habit because of you. But when it comes to our marriage..." His gaze was raw with unhidden emotion. "I couldn't bear to risk losing you. Never again."

"Not ever." I held his gaze. "No matter what you want, I swear I won't hold it against you. Even if it conflicts with my dreams, I *know* we can sort it out somehow, working together."

"Well..." His eyes lowered, long eyelashes shadowing his lean brown cheeks. "I *have* had an idea of my own," he said. "But if it diminished one of your dreams... I couldn't bear it if you said yes only because—"

"*Wrexham.*" I nudged his shoulder gently. "Just tell me!"

He took a deep breath, looking down at the sheets between us. "I'm not like you." His voice was quiet but steady. "I love magic itself, but I never dreamed of fame and public acclaim as you did. My dreams were exactly what you grew up taking for granted. A family all collected in one place. Enough money for everyone I love to be safe. A home full of people whom I love."

"And you don't think you can have that now?" A half-laugh startled out of me. "Look around at this house!

What do you think I've been designing for us here, if not that?"

As his eyes flashed back to mine, the sheer vulnerability in his expression stopped my breath. "But this school is *your* dream," he said softly. "And you never invited me to share in it. Not even once. I kept hoping that you would, in time, but—"

"Oh, for—!" A half-sob fell from my throat as I sat up straight, staring down at him in disbelief. "*Of course* I never asked you to work at Thornfell. How could I? I was afraid you would feel that you *had* to agree—and then you'd lose your own future and all of your dreams. You know you'd be slashed from the Great Library's register of alumni if you worked here—just as I was, and Luton, too. How could *I* be the one to ask you for that?"

He frowned up at me. "But—"

"I want you to have everything *you* want," I said firmly. "The fact that this school started as my dream doesn't mean it has to belong only to me forever. It's already being shared by all of my students. And do you have *any idea* how badly I could use a second professor of magic? Then I wouldn't have to teach every class but weather wizardry and run myself ragged every day! To have another magician I could truly trust here—much less someone who could teach my students, from experience, the real, practical work that an officer of magic does—"

"So you *are* inviting me to work here with you and build this dream together after all?" My husband's lips began to curve as he rose to meet me eye-to-eye, one hand settling gently on my closest shoulder. "Is that what you're saying to me, right now, Harwood? And was that your idea for how we could solve things tonight, even before I told you what I wanted?"

"Well, of course it was! But I was afraid you would only agree for my sake, so..." I shook my head ruefully. "Oh, my love. Have you ever noticed that both of us are good at understanding magic but rather hopeless at understanding other people?"

Wrexham looked at me for a long moment, as intensely as if he were memorizing every detail. Then: "No," he said firmly. "I'm afraid you're wrong, Harwood. *Completely* wrong, in fact. *Entirely* mistaken."

"I am?" I blinked.

His eyes glittered dangerously in the candlelight. "We *are* both good at magic," he told me, "and we will run an *excellent* school together.

"*However...*" My husband's lips curved into a triumphantly wicked grin as he gave my shoulder a sudden, gentle push and tumbled me, off-guard, onto my back on the mattress of our bed.

My breath caught as I lost my balance. Wrexham shifted fluidly above me, caging my shoulders between his arms. His dark gaze blazed into mine, fierce with joy and wonder —and *all* mine, forever, with no more horrible, endless separations forced between us.

"I think you'll find, darling Harwood," he murmured, his breath warm against my skin, "that we understand one another in an *extremely* vital and personal way. If, as my new headmistress, you would allow me a practical demonstration of that point...?"

Golden candlelight shone from the side table, lighting the hollows of my husband's lean cheeks and his shining dark hair above me.

I wrapped my fingers around his shoulders and arched luxuriantly against him. Magic tingled in the air. A shining future stretched before us, full of more dazzling possibilities than I'd ever dreamed possible.

"Go on then," I dared, and felt his breathing quicken in response. Over all these years, we had always risen to each other's challenges. "Why don't you prove it to me...if you can?"

He did.

Thoroughly.

WHAT COMES NEXT

Thank you so much to everyone who's read this second volume of Cassandra's story! You've probably already read Volume I, but if you haven't, you can catch up on the Harwood Spellbook by going back to Volume I, *Snowspelled.*

If you'd like to read the story of Amy and Jonathan's own romance, you can read my prequel novella *Spellswept* (set in the Harwoods' famous underwater ballroom).

You may not be surprised to learn that Miss Banks and Miss Fennell jointly star in the next novella in this series. (And yes, *of course* they'll get a happy ending. My heroines always do!) Their story, *Moontangled*, will come out on February 3rd, 2020.

If you'd like to stay up-to-date with future stories in this series (and others)—*and* get the chance to read free tie-in short stories and win advance copies of future books!—please do sign up to my newsletter:

www.stephanieburgis.com/newsletter

You can get early copies of my ebooks and read my monthly Dragons' Book Club column (where my readers trade fabulous recs of their own!) at my Patreon:

www.patreon.com/stephanieburgis

And if you have the time and energy to review *Thornbound* online, I would be incredibly grateful. Word-of-mouth makes a huge difference to the life of a series, and I'd love to keep on playing in this world for as long as possible. Thank you!

SPELLSWEPT

A PREQUEL TO THE HARWOOD SPELLBOOK

I n the world of the Harwood Spellbook, 19th-century Angland is ruled by a powerful group of women known as the Boudiccate—but in order to become a member of that elite group, any ambitious young politician must satisfy tradition by taking a gentleman mage for her husband.

Amy Standish is a born politician...but Jonathan Harwood is her greatest temptation. On the night of the Harwoods' Spring Solstice Ball, in an underwater ballroom full of sparkling fey lights and danger, Amy will have to fight the greatest political battle of her life to win a family and a future that she could never have imagined.

It will take an entirely unexpected kind of magic to keep everything from crashing down around her.

Warning: this novella contains forbidden romance, dangerous magic, and political intrigue in an underwater ballroom. What could possibly go wrong?

ACKNOWLEDGMENTS

Thank you to my fearless and steadfast beta readers: Rene Sears, Patrick Samphire, and Jenn Reese. You guys kept me going through every stage, and I appreciated it SO MUCH.

Thank you to everyone who generously read and critiqued *Thornbound* despite the fact that I sent it to them at one of the busiest times of the year: Tiffany Trent, Leah Cypess, Claire Fayers, David Burgis, Aliette de Bodard, and Patrick Samphire. I am so grateful for the help!

Thank you to everyone who answered my call for help on Facebook when I needed to know more about the sounds of the woods at night: Sorrel Jones, Helen Hall, Helen Fairbank, Neil Beynon, Karen Ball, Suzanne McLeod, Emma Pass, Anthony McGowan, and Jaime Lee Moyer. Any leftover inaccuracies (that can't be explained by fey magic!) are entirely my own fault.

Thank you to Leesha Hannigan for the gorgeous cover art, and for being so patient and flexible along the way. Thank you to Patrick Samphire for the speedy and fabulous cover design—it is *so* useful to be married to a wonderful cover designer! (And next time, I promise I'll bake you vegan chocolate-chip cookies as a thank-you.)

Thank you so much to Tiffany Trent for careful copy-editing, support, and friendship. Thank you to eagle-eyed early readers Melita Kennedy, Xenia Tashlitsky and Becky Browne for helping me clean up errors that I'd introduced post-copyedits.

And thank you to my older son, who forced me to break up my rewriting sessions to watch fun episodes of *Kim Possible* with him *and* told me he was sure that this book would be good. I truly appreciated both parts!

Printed in Great Britain
by Amazon